JANET PYWELL

The Concealers

A Ronda George Thriller - Book 1

In memory of Ronda Evett.

Grateful thanks to Julia Gibbs, Tommy Smith and Frankie Smith from the Whitstable Kickboxing Sports Club and Amanda for all her love and support.

Foreword

The Concealers
Book 1

A Ronda George Thriller
Talented kickboxer and *Masterchef* turns detective.

Betrayed, bankrupt and broken – Can Ronda get back in the game?

After her ex-boyfriend's stolen her savings and confidence, Ronda George is desperate to get back in the game. When she's employed to cater for a private 50th birthday party at a Castle in Scotland, she also agrees to be the 'eyes and ears' for Inspector Joachin García Abascal from Europol.

But the family have their secrets and are concealing truths involving an unsolved murder and a stolen rare blue diamond.

What should be a simple catering job turns into a nightmare as enemies are bent on revenge. Ronda must use all the skills from her military career to stay alive.

The *Concealers* is the first book in the Ronda George series of thrillers which can be read and enjoyed in any order, although it's exciting to watch Ronda's personal development with each book in the series and it's preferable to read them in sequence.

Fans of female sleuths and aficionados of Lucy Foley, Catherine Cooper, Allie Reynolds, Shari Lapena, Riley Sager and Lisa Jewell.

Chapter 1

"A fault is fostered by concealment."
Virgil

Herr Schiltz looks like my late father.

Unfortunately, we didn't get on, especially after he emotionally blackmailed me into a career at Sandhurst. Officer material, he called me. It wasn't what I wanted, not Sandhurst nor the army. But after my mother died and I'd grown out of boarding school, I didn't have the fight left in me to argue with Brigadier Charles George.

Sadly, in the end it wasn't what he wanted either – nothing was ever prestigious enough, not even when I rose to the rank of captain.

Like my late father, Herr Schiltz is late-sixties maybe seventy with severely combed-back thin, white hair and a pencil moustache that's reminiscent of a sixties screen idol. Only there's something cold in his eyes, and I suspect that Herr Schiltz, as was my father, is very used to getting his own way.

He points at a single uncomfortable chair opposite his desk in his flashy modern, glass and chrome London office that has about as much soul as my dead father with its lemon-scented air freshener.

'Sit down, Ronda.'

He doesn't smile, and suddenly, I'm reminded of that day in my father's study, when I told him I wanted to become a world-class chef. His face had clouded over and his eyes were thunderous and angry.

'I haven't invested in you to work in a blasted kitchen.'

'I'd be a Michelin chef,' I argued.

'You're going to Sandhurst – that's the end of it. Now, get out!'

Herr Schiltz checks through the papers on his desk, and when he looks up, I straighten my back.

'Well, Ronda George, you come highly recommend.'

'Thank you.'

'It says here that you left the British army in 2017 and you went on to win *Masterchef* – a television programme in the United Kingdom – two years ago.' He speaks perfect English without a trace of a German accent.

'Yes.'

'And since then?'

'I've been catering for private functions: parties, banquettes, private dining at specific venues and events—'

'Including William and Kate?'

'I have cooked for several members of the royal family – in a private capacity.'

'I'd imagine they're quite fussy?'

'I don't speak about my clients, but I do have permission to list them.'

'Good. Good. I need total discretion.' He stares at me, taking in my short, spiky, black hair and my deep-set green eyes – my mother's legacy.

I pull at the hem of my navy Chanel suit I bought especially for these type of interviews then grip my shaking fingers together in my lap. Sandhurst had promised me 'Confidence that lasts a lifetime'; they didn't lie but they couldn't foresee what would happen.

'I want you for the whole weekend.'

'That's fine,' my voice croaks.

'Did Paula give you the date?'

'Your secretary said it would be in a few weeks, around mid-August.'

'You can arrive ahead of the party. There will be ten of us – all adults thankfully no children – arriving Friday evening until Sunday night. You can leave on Monday morning. There will be housekeepers and staff in the kitchen who will help you, and a sommelier – you can work with them all. They're used to fine-dining catering so you won't have any problems. My chauffeur Jim will also be there.'

'Perfect.'

'I'll fly you up there.'

'What? I assumed you wanted me here in—'

'London?' He laughs. 'Heavens, no. It's a special occasion. Scotland. It's my wife's fiftieth birthday, and I'm flying the family and some friends up there as a surprise – Calder Castle. Have you heard of it?'

'Er, no.'

'Didn't Paula tell you?'

'I haven't met Paula, but we did speak on the phone.'

Paula had been as aloof and unfriendly as Herr Schiltz.

'Can you make a birthday cake?'

'Yes.'

'She likes vanilla sponge.'

'No problem.'

'Make an effort – it has to be special – not too big or expensive but something to do with golf,' he adds vaguely.

'Of course.'

'You can liaise with Paula. She will see to everything.'

I don't reply. I'm busy wondering who will look after Molly for the weekend. It's not easy to find someone to look after a boisterous and lively two-year-old—

'Is there a problem, Ronda?'

I shake my head.

'It's fine.'

I'll worry about Molly later. This job is too good to turn down, and I need the money – much more than anyone could imagine.

'Right.' Herr Schiltz stands up. 'I want you to submit a variety of menus for the entire weekend, including some vegetarian and vegan options. I suppose some of the family will have gone on those sorts of diets by now, and once I sign off on them, you can order the food in advance. Liaise with the housekeeper up there, she will organise everything you need and if you're stuck, ask Paula.'

I nod my head. 'Is there anything in particular you'd like me to prepare?'

'Fish, salmon, source everything locally – Scottish, of course.'

'Of course.'

'Right, you can go now. I have another appointment.' Herr Schiltz stands up, but he doesn't look at me. He consults his diary that lies open on the glass table, runs his finger down the page and taps his finger against a name then reaches for his phone.

He looks up surprised I'm still seated.

I get to my feet and glance around the double-aspect office

with views of Canary Wharf below then I take a deep breath to control my shaking voice.

'Herr Schiltz, what about my remuneration for the week-end?'

He frowns, and his mouth with his pencil moustache turns down at the corner.

'You'll be well-paid, and if our guests are pleased, there's also a bonus for you.'

'How much—'

He holds up his hand. 'I don't discuss money. It's vulgar. Speak to my secretary.'

Then like I did fifteen years ago leaving my father's study, I tiptoe from his office wondering if I'm doing the right thing but realising that I have no choice.

On this occasion, I desperately need the money.

* * *

I lead with my left foot, throwing punches with my dominant right hand. Then I follow this with more robust energy with my non-dominant hand and lean forward in a boxing stance punching faster and faster until I'm breathless and the sweat drips from my forehead.

I see James's face and his smiling blue eyes.

I thump the bag again and hit him between the eyes.

I do ten side kick squats then I place my legs either side of the punch bag and catch my breath before doing a sit-up and punching the bag ten more times.

I'm panting hard. Thumping, timed, rhythmic, repeating, smacking, hitting, swearing in my head at James – my ex.

'Working on your core strength?' Tina asks.

'Pain,' I grunt. 'Inflicting pain.'

'James again?'

'Yep.' I pause, panting and gasping, and reach for my water bottle.

'Taking out your frustration?'

'Yep.'

Tina, my best friend, is wearing a rainbow T-shirt and shorts that show off her slender legs. She grins at me and hides behind the punchbag.

'Want to practise with me?'

'I thought you'd never ask.' I grin and rise to my feet, adjusting my red tank top and long sweat pants. 'Uppercut?' I smile, rotating my torso and bringing my fist upward striking the punch bag, then again and again. Kickboxing is the best sport for me; it combines honing my physical strength with my current mental desire for inflicting pain.

'Need to talk?' Tina holds the punch bag unflinching.

I bring my fists to my face in a fighting stance and shift my weight to my right foot. I bring my left knee up to my chest, foot flexed, and my heel close to my gluteus then I kick out my left foot – straight from the hip – leading with the heel, inches from Tina's chest then I bring my foot to the floor and retain my fighting stance.

'This kickboxing is thirsty work,' Tina says, turning away and grabbing her sweatshirt. 'Come on. I'll buy you a gin. You look like you need one.'

* * *

'Could you do me a huge favour, Tina? Say you'll look after Molly. It's only for a long weekend. You know she adores you.' She places two gin and tonics on the pub table where I'm sitting in the corner cooling down near the open windows. Outside a group of businessmen have loosened the buttons on their shirts. Their jackets are draped over the pub benches.

She glances through the open sash window where buckets of colourful petunias are in flower. 'All the tables are full outside; you were lucky to get this one.'

'Are you avoiding my question?' I ask. 'Please, Tina. There isn't anyone else I can ask.'

'That's because she's spoilt and greedy.'

'How dare you say that. She's affectionate and loving.'

I suppress a lasting memory of Tina and Molly, my labradoodle, play-wrestling on the sofa last week. She covered Tina in great big wet sloppy licks and Tina said she hated it when Molly licked her, but I suspect she secretly loved the attention.

'Well, she's that too but—'

'Oh, Tina, come on. You're my best friend.'

'I'm your only friend.'

'Okay, that's probably true.'

'You could ask James?' Tina suggests with a sly smile.

'You know I'm never speaking to him again, besides it's his fault that I'm in this mess anyway.'

'I thought you loved him—'

'I did, but I never thought he'd—'

I break off, unable to finish the sentence. I'm not sure if I'm angry with him or myself. Why did I always end up in such a mess?

'Look, Ronda. I told you not to give him thirty thousand pounds—'

I hold up the palm of my hand. 'I know, but it's too late now, Tina. Look, I … I need the money. Oh God, what a mess, I'm bankrupt.'

'Will you get any of it back?'

'He said he was looking for a job, but now he's disappeared. He's a liar. That's why I can't turn down Herr Schiltz.'

'Alright, I'll take Molly.'

'Thank you.' I pause. 'I hope I can do it, Tina. I haven't cooked professionally for months.'

'It's like riding a bicycle.' Tina grins.

'He's a brute.'

'A brute?' Tina grins and imitates a bad Scottish accent. 'Are you being a wee bit dramatic, lassie?'

'He's just like my dad.'

'Ah, so is that what got you so fired up in the gym? You were even angrier today than normal.'

'Probably.'

'Well, that's not a good sign.'

I gaze at Tina. She has known me since we were both six, and we went to primary school together. Now, at thirty-three, she looks younger than me, slimmer than me, and prettier than me. Tina is the opposite of me in every single way; her clothes and hair are neat. She's organised and calm. She attends yoga and meditation classes and holds down a respectable job as a criminal lawyer with a prestigious London law firm.

'You could try counselling?' she suggests.

'That's not an option,' I say, dismissively. 'Would you believe, Herr Schiltz even has the same pencil moustache,' I grumble.

'Gosh, how awful.' Tina grins; unlike my flawed face that shows frown lines on my forehead and crow's feet at the corner of my eyes, her skin is perfect. She has a heart-shaped face, a dimpled chin and long blonde hair. 'It's no wonder you were punching the bag like a maniac on the loose.'

'I like to think I have more style than that.' I pause, and a shiver runs down my spine. 'Herr Schiltz did say I came highly recommended.'

'Well of course you do, Ronda. You're famous. Think of all the people you've cooked for since you won that Bake-Off programme,' she teases.

'*Masterchef* – it was *Masterchef* – and I'm not famous, besides I've worked bloody hard to build my clientele.'

'I hardly saw you for two years,' Tina complains. 'You were always hobnobbing with royalty; it was either Charles or Camilla, or the Beckhams when they're in London, or that singer—'

'Sam Smith.'

'Look,' Tina says, leaning forward. 'It was a blip. You lost your confidence, that's all. It was temporary.'

'I was a wreck. I ruined the food and burnt half of it, and I still don't know if I can—'

'Of course, you can. You'll be fine.'

I shake my head. 'After seeing his office—'

'You won't be cooking in his office. You're going to Scotland.'

'He's rented a castle for the weekend – Castle Calder. There's a whole programme of events – including a shooting morning – that his secretary sent to me, and I have to plan the meals for ten guests for the entire weekend.' I nod at my gym bag on the floor not daring to bring out the list of requirements.

'Who's he shooting?' Tina laughs.

'Grouse – I think it's the season, or deer or rabbits? I don't know, Tina. I wish I didn't have to go. His secretary is young and miserable. It wouldn't surprise me if she had steel caps on her shoes and on top of that when I called the housekeeper, she sounded dour and resentful.' I drain my glass.

'And you haven't even arrived yet.' Tina laughs. 'This will be so exciting, and it will do you good to get away.'

Tina has always propped me up, made me laugh. We egg each other on, try and keep upbeat and positive. It has kept us going through the traumas of our lives: school, exams, university, boyfriends, family and jobs as well as a multitude of heartaches and breakups – although they've mostly been mine as a result of me not choosing wisely: Wrong career – Sandhurst. Wrong employer – British Army. Wrong boyfriend – James.

'When do you go?' Tina breaks my thoughtful spell.

'Next weekend. The 12th of August.'

'That's short notice for his wife's fiftieth birthday. Is it his second wife?'

'He must be almost seventy, so I guess so.'

'Are you making a cake?'

'He mentioned a golf theme, but who knows? I'm still waiting to hear back on the list of menus I've suggested for the whole weekend. I've just submitted the fifth suggestions.' I rub my tired eyes.

'Once you're there and you've met everyone in person, you'll be fine.'

I grin. 'You know me, once I'm in the kitchen I'm at my happiest, it's all the other crap you have to deal with that I'm not good at.'

Tina drains her glass.

'Another one?' I ask. At least I can afford it now. With the promise of earning a month's salary for working a long weekend, I suddenly feel like celebrating.

'Of course.' She smiles and hands me her empty glass. 'And, don't get me any of that crappy diet tonic.'

It's been a long-standing joke between us that she drinks

ordinary tonic and is a dress size smaller than me.

'I think I'll go for the full-fat tonic now that James isn't here to remind me constantly that I have to lose weight. By the way, how's Graham?'

'Graham and I are having a break for a while. It's been a bit intense and working in the same office, you know, it can be a little claustrophobic.'

'Is he still jogging with you?'

'I take a different route most mornings now.'

'I wish I was like you, Tina. You juggle your work and men so effortlessly.'

'You need to practise, Ronda. Maybe you'll find a handsome Scotsman and fall in love.'

'Knowing my luck, Herr Schiltz's family and friends will be equally as obnoxious as he is, and the kitchen staff at the castle will be rude and difficult, and I'll come back exhausted vowing never to cook again.'

'Think of the money,' Tina says, laughing. 'You'll be able to give it all away to the next man you meet.'

I poke my tongue out at her.

'I can't help it if I'm over-generous. It comes from years of being financially controlled by Brigadier Charles George.' I give a mock salute. 'All the years of hearing my father say he wasn't giving me money, and it doesn't grow on trees, and everything had to have a monetary value... I'm rebelling, Tina.'

'You should have escaped to Australia like Francis.'

I smile, thinking of my younger brother who I chat with regularly on Skype, looking happily sun-tanned and, like me, still single.

'Think positively, Ronda. Since your father passed away three years ago, you've left the army, and you won *Masterchef*.

Stay focused. Don't put yourself down. Remember, that inside that reticent and thoughtful head of yours is a kind and loving friend – sometimes too trusting but nevertheless generous.'

'I'm not falling in love anymore. I'm staying celibate for five years and that way I don't have to trust anyone.'

'See that bloke at the bar is staring at you.' Tina nudges me, and we both know full well that the older, handsome stranger – probably European – can't take his eyes off Tina. She's stunning.

'Then you'd better get the drinks,' I say, opening my purse. 'I don't trust myself to be nice to him or anyone.' I pass her a twenty-pound note.

Tina stands up and pulls down the hem of her skirt. She whispers seductively and giggles, 'I won't be long, baby.'

But before she can move the good-looking man is already standing at our table. He's dressed casually in navy chinos and a crisp linen shirt, and his dark eyes are bewitching. He holds his hand out to me and speaks with a trace of a Spanish accent.

'Ronda George, forgive me for approaching you in a pub like this. My name is Inspector Joachin García Abascal.'

Chapter 2

'The same words conceal and declare the thoughts of men.'
Alfred Lord Tennyson

'May I buy you ladies a drink?' he asks.

Tina twists her long blonde hair flirtatiously between her fingers. Old habits never die. But Inspector Joachin García Abascal is looking directly at me.

'We were just leaving,' I lie.

He looks amused and pulls out a stool to sit beside me. 'I would like to speak to you on police business. I'm not here to, er, how do you say? Hit on you?'

'Police business?' Tina's criminal and legal experience kicks in, and she sits down quickly, so the three of us are seated around the small table. 'What does that have to do with Ronda?'

'Well, this is what I wanted to speak to her about, confidentially, of course.'

I'm uncomfortable under his gaze, but I can't take my eyes from his face. He seems too kind, open and friendly to be a police officer.

From the corner of my eye, I see Tina nod seriously, encouraging him. Why doesn't she ask him to leave us alone?

'If you'll spare me a few minutes to explain, Ronda, I'd be grateful, please?'

I can't breathe, and I'm tongue-tied. I gaze at my hands in my lap.

Fortunately, Tina doesn't share the same traits as me because she leans forward and whispers, 'Do you have any identification, inspector?'

He reaches into his back pocket and pulls out a worn leather wallet with an ID card. 'Of course, and please call me Joachin.'

'Europol?' Tina questions as she scrutinises the ID card.

'Yes. I'm with the International Crime Squad at Europol. Mostly, I specialise in tracking down stolen antiquities in Europe, but we work closely with all the criminal intelligence agencies within the European police forces. We have no jurisdiction here in the UK, and we can't arrest anyone or carry out investigations without the approval of each country's authorities.'

'So you'd need the British authority, here in England?'

'That's right.' His smile is disarming, and I smile back, impressed with the way he speaks. 'But we work closely with the British police to fight international crime; human trafficking, money laundering, terrorism, cybercrime and drugs, things like that.' He shrugs and raises his shoulders in the Mediterranean way of speaking. 'We want to keep everyone safe.'

He turns his attention to me and smiles.

'So why do you want to speak to Ronda?' Tina asks, determined not to be left out.

'We know that you have been asked to cater for a small party next weekend at Castle Calder near Aberdeen.'

I gasp, surprised and flattered that I'm of interest to someone.

'You know about that?'

He smiles reassuringly. 'We haven't been following you or anything like that, but we are concerned about the man who has employed you, Herr Schiltz.'

'I'm not surprised,' I say before I can stop myself. 'He's no good.' I shake my head.

The inspector tilts his head to one side. 'Why do you say that?'

I glance at Tina for support, but she's staring at me with her legal gaze, and I stumble over my words when I explain.

'Well, I found him intimidating, not friendly, not nice or …'

Tina adds helpfully, 'He's like her father, who was a narcissistic bully. A brigadier in the army. He wasn't a kind man.'

The inspector nods in understanding. 'I can imagine, my father was also a complicated man.'

'Really?' I ask eagerly; it seems surprising that this charming Spaniard could have had anything awful happen in his life.

The inspector clasps his hands together and rests his elbows on the table. 'I'd like to tell you a little about Herr Schiltz, if I may?'

'Only if you buy us a drink – gin,' Tina quips, but without missing a beat, and smiling, the inspector rises to his feet and walks to the bar.

'What are you doing?' I hiss, 'I thought we were trying to get rid of him.'

'I want to speak to you, Ronda. I need to know what's going on?' Tina whispers urgently.

I lean across the table, and before I reply, I glance over my shoulder to make sure he isn't looking at us.

'I know as much as you,' I say.

'What do you know about Herr bloody Schiltz?' she insists.

'Nothing.'

'You haven't Googled him, or read anything about him?'

'No.'

'Why not?'

'I never thought about it. I went to his office in Canary Wharf. There didn't seem to be any need to Google him too.'

'What does he do?'

I shrug. 'Investments? Property? Banking?'

'Oh God, Ronda. I thought you were much smarter than this. Shush, here he comes.'

The inspector places the small tray on the table and hands out the gin and tonics. 'I ordered us doubles, as they're not worth drinking otherwise.' He smiles and sits down. '*Salud.*'

We raise our glasses.

'Cheers.'

'So, let me tell you about Herr Schiltz without boring you too much.' He wipes his top lip with his slim fingers. 'The Schiltz family made a lot of money after the Second World War in Germany. They rose quickly to the top of high society, financing new projects and buildings in different German cities. They helped repair many of the country's cultural sites that had been destroyed by the Allies and, by the time Friedrich Schiltz – the man you met – was born in the 50s, his family was already wealthy. Since then Friedrich has continued, successfully growing the family business. He has become a well-known philanthropist in Germany and maybe in some other parts of the world.'

'That's good.' I nod at Tina as if to say, *Herr Schiltz can't be that bad, and I didn't need to Google him after all.*

'However…' The inspector leans forward. 'His wife was found dead in their home in Berlin.'

I cover my mouth with my hand and say, 'But I'm cooking for his wife's fiftieth birthday.'

'You are, but you are cooking for his second wife, Louisa. Rumour has it that they were having an affair years before his first wife was found dead.'

'How did wife number one die?' asks Tina.

'Iris was murdered. Shot. But unfortunately, the murder weapon was never found.'

'How long ago?'

'Five years ago.'

'Who did it?' Tina's like a dog with a bone and I can imagine her thoroughness at work.

The inspector shrugs. 'The police don't know. A man was arrested. He was a friend of the family and the gardener. Friedrich maintained that his wife was having an affair with him. He suggested that she wanted to end their relationship, but the man was jealous of her living with her husband, so – this man shot her.'

'Did he get a prison sentence?'

'Yes, he got fifteen years, but he died after one year in prison. He killed himself.'

'Goodness.' I take a gulp of my strong gin, grateful for the refreshing lime.

'He maintained his innocence until the end.'

'That's tragic,' I whisper.

'So, why are you here?' Tina toys with the slice of lime in her glass and the inspector watches her fish it out. She proceeds to bite into the bitter flesh as she asks, 'What does this have to do with Ronda?'

'We've been watching Herr Schiltz for a while. He's made most of his money with investments and, over the years, he has invested in several valuable artefacts—'

'Like paintings?'

'Yes. Exactly. He purchased many valuable objects; paintings, statues and similar things, as investments on behalf of several banks.' The inspector sips his drink, and the ice cubes rattle noisily against the glass.

'However, that's not all. Last year, you may remember there was severe flooding in many parts of Europe and in Germany, some houses and properties were washed away. Unfortunately, several businesses were also affected, and in particular when the Rhine burst its riverbank, ironically it swept away several properties including – a bank.'

'One of the banks that Herr Schiltz's had worked with?'

The inspector looks at Tina and nods gravely. 'Yes. Fortunately, some of the valuable artwork was rescued and can be restored. But the strength of the river, the flooding water, took away the foundations of the bank and the cellars. It meant the safety deposit boxes were swept off in the current and some of their contents were never located.'

'Goodness,' I whisper, imagining the resulting mess of the filthy water. I remember how our TV screens had been full of floods in the north of England, showing the devastation of houses and people's lives. Seemingly it took years to get rid of the stench and stains left by muddy water, and many families weren't covered by insurance.

The inspector continues, 'You can imagine how it is, the banks have a fundamental duty to look after the valuable items placed under their care. Many owners of the deposit boxes don't want to tell the authorities what's inside the boxes because sometimes they contain illegal items, or they have been acquired under, what shall we say…' He looks at Tina and adds, 'Mitigating circumstances.'

I realise that the inspector has done his homework. He's approached us when we are together, and he knows that my best friend, Tina, is a criminal lawyer. I also think he knows that he can trust us both.

He takes a deep breath.

'I'll be honest with you; not everyone even tells their family what's inside the vaults. It could be money, a painting, jewellery or something of similar value. Perhaps even a stolen object, bought on the black market, that they keep safe in the bank deposit boxes. They wait for the fuss to die down before they can bring it back out again and try and sell it on. Some people often exchange stolen artefacts for drug money or human cargo—'

'Do you mean trafficking?' asks Tina.

'Unfortunately yes, many groups or operations that specialise in bringing workers from one country to the next for illegal work, do so by forcing or coercing naive people. They pretend they are going to better lives. They are invariably coerced into the illicit sex trade, or swapped for drugs or some awful life in another country or on another continent where they don't even speak the language.'

'That's awful,' I whisper.

'Yes, Ronda. It's terrible, and it's my job to stop it.' His chestnut eyes with their long dark lashes are intensely serious.

'Is Herr Schiltz muddled up with all this?' Tina asks.

The inspector smiles and raises a hand. 'No, we have no proof that he's involved in the illegal trafficking of drugs or humans.'

'Then what do you want with me, inspector?' I ask.

'Please, call me Joachin.'

'Joachin.' His name rolls off my tongue like delicious rich, dark, seductive chocolate.

'Well, as I said, one of the deposit boxes that Herr Schiltz registered as missing, and this wouldn't normally be anything to be concerned about, but the contents of the box were insured for a large sum of money—'

'Which he claimed?' Tina asks.

'Yes.'

'So what's the problem?'

'Nine items were listed, and only eight were claimed on the insurance.'

'How do you know this?' Tina asks.

Inspector Joachin smiles when he replies, 'Unfortunately, I can't tell you.'

I say, not wanting Tina to get all the attention, 'So you're looking for something Herr Schiltz had in a deposit box – in a bank safety deposit box – that has gone missing, swept away in the flooding last year.'

'Potentially swept away... exactly.'

'And what is it?' I ask.

'Well, this is our problem – we're not sure. But we do believe it's one of the reasons he's organising this party next weekend, for all his family and friends. We believe that the missing item is relevant to them all.'

'Why?'

'Again, we don't know. It's a shot in the dark admittedly, but what we do know is that eight missing items have been traced and recovered.'

'Really?' I'm surprised. 'How?'

'Because he was willing to give the insurance company a detailed description of those articles and the recovery team have been diligent in the process of their rescue.'

'So why worry, it's just one more thing, isn't it? And besides, if he doesn't want to claim on the insurance, then it doesn't matter. He must have lots of money anyway.' I finish my drink, place the glass on the table and check my watch. 'Molly needs to go out,' I say to Tina, but she ignores me.

'What's the ninth item?' she asks.

The inspector's eyes are dark and serious when he answers. 'That's what we need to find out.'

'Is it stolen?' asks Tina.

'Yes and probably extremely valuable.'

'So what do you want me to do?' I bite my lip.

Joachin smiles, and his wedding band glistens in the sunlight streaming through the pub's open window.

'Nothing dangerous, I'd like you to simply be my eyes and ears.'

I smile back, and for some peculiar reason, I think this has to be the most straightforward task in the world. Nothing will happen in a kitchen.

* * *

The early morning flight lands effortlessly with barely a small bump and squeal of brakes at Aberdeen airport. As the propellers whine and the plane taxis to the terminal, I pull out the itinerary for the Schiltz's Scottish birthday weekend. Tonight, Friday night, there's a welcome dinner – a buffet – and on Saturday night is Mrs Schiltz's birthday celebration. The last time I'd attended a birthday celebration for a friend of James, he'd been very drunk, and I'd found him kissing a young girl in the bathroom.

It didn't bode well and for some reason, the thought of being here in Scotland, in the middle of the summer, suddenly fills me with dread. I have a fleeting suspicion that something is going to go terribly wrong.

I collect my bags and head into the arrivals hall. My mouth is dry, and my head is thumping from the tension spreading across my shoulders.

What if I can't cook?

'Ronda George?'

I turn at the sound of my name pronounced with a Scottish accent.

'Hello.'

'I'm Mac. I'm here to collect you.'

'Thank you.' I hold out my hand, but he ignores it and reaches for my wheelie suitcase.

'Can you manage your other bag?' he asks gruffly.

I hitch my rucksack over my shoulder. 'Yes, thank you.'

'Follow me.'

Outside the summer air is cold, and there's a smell of plane fuel on the breeze that floats across the car park.

'It's a beautiful day,' I say.

He points at a grey Range Rover. 'We're over there.'

Mac opens the boot and doesn't look at me as he speaks. 'It's thirty minutes to Castle Calder.'

'Thank you. Have you lived here all your life?'

'No.'

I climb into the passenger seat and on the journey, Mac rebuffs my questions and doesn't speak. I study his profile; deep-set eyes, short brown hair and tidy beard. He's older than me; probably late forties but I'm soon distracted, and I gaze out of the car window at the glorious countryside, rich with green ferns in the early morning sunshine. I'm wondering what kitchen facilities the castle has when Mac says, 'It's another ten minutes.'

'Thank you for collecting me.'

'You couldn't walk.'

'That's true. Not if they want their dinner tonight and not on Monday.'

He grins, revealing a small gap between his front teeth. 'Do you know Scotland?'

'Not this part.'

I've only been to Scotland once before, to Glasgow, with James. It had been a disaster. I should have realised after he left his credit card at home, and I'd paid for the hotel, dinner, shopping and treats, that he was deceitful and a liar.

'Castle Calder is one of a kind.' Mac indicates and turns the steering wheel of the Range Rover with ease to overtake a lorry heading north.

'Have you worked there long?'

'My mother is the housekeeper.'

'Mrs Long?' I ask.

She was the woman I spoke to on the phone. Her manner was brusque to the point of rudeness. I was dreading meeting her and worse still, working in her kitchen.

'That's her. She can be short, and it sometimes seems as if she's rude, but she isn't. Don't take anything she says personally, Ronda.' He smiles and gives me a sidelong glance. 'I hope you're made of stern stuff.'

'I'm like the Tin Man – only I'm a woman.'

He laughs. 'I'll bear that in mind.'

'How many are in the kitchen?'

'Erm, let's see.' He frowns. 'There's Mum, Julie, and Dan.

He's not from around here either.'

'What do you do, Mac?'

'Everything. I'm the estate manager so I'll be carrying their bags, I'll organise the grouse hunting in the morning and just about anything else that needs doing. We all have to pitch in. You'll have to help too.'

'I'll be helping, Mac. I'm cooking, remember? I'm not on holiday.'

Mac grins. 'I think you'll get on alright with Mum.'

'What do you know about the guests?'

'Mr and Mrs Schiltz? Nothing really – apart from they've more money than sense. They're paying over the odds for everything – a ridiculous sum of money for the weekend – and they don't care. They don't even notice the money. It's as if they know they'll never run out of it. I can't imagine how that must feel, you know – to be able to buy what you want without a thought, without worrying about the price of anything. It doesn't fit with our Scottish way.' He grins.

'Ah yes, you're notoriously thrifty, you Scots – if it's still politically correct to say so.'

Mac's laugh is a deep rumble. 'You can say it with me, but I'd bide your tongue in the kitchen with Mum. Now, here we are, this is the start of the long drive that leads to the front entrance.' He nods at a narrow sandy-coloured driveway, with manicured lawns on each side leading to open fields and a forest beyond. 'Do you want to walk it? We normally let the guests off here, and John, the gardener, plays the pipes to welcome them.'

'No, that's fine. You can drive me to the front door, thanks. It looks a pretty long drive.'

'It's a quarter of a mile.'

'It looks like a fairy tale castle – a French château.'

'That's why it's a popular corporate and wedding venue. The turrets, gables and balustrades date back to 1575. There are over eighty acres of gardens and woodlands, and in the gardens, there is space outside for outdoor activities, picnics and alfresco dining. Are you listening to me, Ronda?'

'Yes, of course,' I reply, but my heart is hammering with excited, child-like enthusiasm. It is simply beautiful. It's striking. I hadn't realised how lovely it would be to leave London and leave all my worries behind. As I step out of the car and into the sunshine, I gaze up at the grey-walled castle with the turrets shining majestically in the sunlight, and a sense of wellbeing and calmness fills my body. Regardless of what the handsome inspector said, and the warnings and caution he gave me, nothing bad could happen here. I suddenly have a very positive feeling. Even the thought of Herr Schiltz and Mrs Long isn't going to faze me. This will be a new beginning.

Chapter 3

'It is the merit of a General to impart good news, and to conceal the truth.'
Sophocles

Mac explains that the French-styled château has four turrets. 'Three of them each contains three bedrooms, a total of nine bedrooms for the ten guests, the chauffeur and the secretary. The fourth turret, nearest the kitchen, has access from the Grand Hall on the ground floor, which is used as the dining room. Above that, is the library. At the top of each turret is a small hall and a corridor which leads out onto the battlements.'

Mac pulls up at the back of the kitchen. The Land Rover stops on the gravel, and I take my bags and follow him along a pretty garden pathway smelling of delicious herbs; thyme, rosemary and sage.

'It's like a secret garden,' I say, feeling excitedly optimistic.

A rugged stone wall protects it, and the winding path leads us to a row of low buildings.

'We converted the stables a few years ago,' Mac explains, pushing open a wooden door. 'But don't hold your breath. They're not luxury.'

He's right. My narrow room has a single bed, a small fridge, a two ringed camping gas stove and a kettle – and there's a miniscule bathroom with a shower cubicle that would barely fit a small child.

'It's not equipped for you to stay here forever.' Mac laughs as I open cupboards with disappointment. 'You're only here for a couple of nights, Ronda.'

'I'm glad this isn't my annual holiday.' I wipe a finger of dust from the mirror hanging on the wall at the foot of the bed.

'The cleaners didn't have time to get to this room. They've been busy preparing the rooms for the big arrival tonight, and between you and me, we're understaffed.'

'And underpaid?' I don't hide the sarcasm in my voice, and he laughs.

'You don't have time to unpack, Mrs Long wants you in the kitchen as soon as possible.'

That's curious. Now we're on the castle grounds he's referring to his mother as Mrs Long.

I close and lock the stable door behind me and pocket the key. 'Who's living in the other four luxury apartments?' I grin.

Mac doesn't smile. 'Julie, the sous chef, is staying here for the weekend, the sommelier Hugo, and Dan, the kitchen boy, until he finds something more permanent in the village.'

'And you?' I smile.

'I live in the converted pig barn over there.' He points to the far side of the estate.

'Living in the height of luxury, are you?' I tease.

He points to a small block of three units. 'It's behind the barn and out of sight and no more luxurious than this.'

'Don't get too used to it then.' I can't hide the sarcasm from my voice.

'I won't, but it's a haven after separating from my ex-wife. I love the peace of it all.'

We walk back through the gardens wordlessly. I'm wondering if the castle is in a similar state of repair and how inadequate the kitchen facilities might be.

He stands aside to let me enter the kitchen, and I'm still absorbing his words as I walk inside and gaze around at the scene before me.

'It's like Downton Abbey,' I say before I have time to think and the words are out of my mouth. I want to ask, where are the modern kitchen appliances? But I manage to stop myself in time as a flustered redhead in her late sixties appears.

'So, you're Ronda,' she says quickly.

There's a lot in the tone of a voice that can make you feel warm, fuzzy or welcome, or it can chill you to the bone with rejection. In this case, Mrs Long, I can sense is not willing to adopt me as her daughter over the coming days, and I'll need to keep my wits about me. I glance for similarities in her and her son, but he's tall and healthy, and she's short and round. They do however share the same straight nose.

'Hello, it's lovely to meet you.' I put on my sincere voice, my best smile and hold out my hand.

'I thought you'd have been here earlier.' She barely takes my hand, but she manages to clasp the tips of my fingers for a second before dropping them as if I'm the devil about to burn her soul.

'The plane was delayed,' Mac lies easily. 'I'll leave you to it.'

I raise an eyebrow, but he winks back at me before sliding out of the kitchen and back toward the garden.

'I'll show you around quickly, but I'm in a hurry there's a lot to do – we're preparing the vegetables, but we need to sort out the meat and the fish.' Mrs Long's rough voice and harsh accent distract me. 'Oh, this is Dan. He's been here a few months. He's an apprentice too.'

Dan is busy peeling potatoes and chucking them into a large pot with a heavy plop. On closer inspection, he's not as young as he looks. There are laughter lines at the corner of his blue eyes, and a patchy beard conceals his narrow face.

I smile wondering what Mrs Long means by saying, he's an apprentice too – but Dan responds with a cheeky wink and I grin back.

'Julie is a cook,' Mrs Long explains.' She's been here a few weeks, and she's promising.'

A ruddy-faced woman with a sparkle in her eyes glances up at me. She's hiding a smile, and busy prepping fish, filleting the salmon with neat professionalism. She waves the blade at me. 'Hello, Ronda.'

'Hi, Julie.' I grin back and raise my hand.

'And Martin helps out washing up.'

Martin waves wet fingers from the sink. He doesn't look sixteen, and I assume it's a summer job where he can earn pocket money in the castle before heading off to university sometime in the future.

'Come on. I'll show you the pantry and the storerooms.' Mrs Long beckons me to follow her down a narrow cold, stone corridor. She points at three doors. 'Pantry. Store. Store.'

In the various storerooms, she pulls out the deliveries and holds them up for inspection. 'Fish – fresh salmon from the harbour, vegetables, fruit and strawberries from the market.' She pops one into her mouth. 'The meat is through here.'

I follow her to the large fridge where she pulls out racks of lamb. 'There's more,' she says. 'There's enough to feed a German army.'

I frown. It's not very PC, but I don't say anything.

Back in the kitchen, I pull my notes from my bag; a detailed notepad, and printed menus and drawings that I've sketched to help me with presentation ideas, all neatly filed in plastics labelled breakfast, lunch, afternoon tea, dinner and supper – the listed ingredients will all be turned into culinary masterpieces.

I lay the menus on the long wooden table in the centre of the kitchen. 'Perhaps we can look at these together, Mrs Long,' I suggest, 'and then we'll both be aware of what needs to be done and we can plan a strategy?'

'I've told the kitchen staff what to do, and we're already organised for tonight's buffet. They know what they're doing.' She folds her arms and stares at me.

'That's good, then let's go over the main points together like, which dishes are proteins, starches, vegetables and salads – and of course, finger food. How many of our guest have confirmed as vegans or vegetarians?'

'I've got a list somewhere,' she replies.

'Great, let's take a look at it. And let's work out how we'll keep the hot dishes, hot.' I smile.

Mrs Long scowls. 'I've been running buffets like these for years, with my eyes closed. We know what we're doing. I've given them all a job.' She waves her arms at Julie, Dan and Martin.

'Fantastic, I can go home then. I gather up my notes.' My patience is getting the better of me. I haven't even been offered a cup of coffee, and my previous good humour has been replaced by one of increasing frustration. I shove my notes inside my bag. 'You can explain to Herr Schiltz why I've left.'

'Well, no, lass, don't be so hasty—'

I raise my voice. 'I haven't been employed specifically by Herr Schiltz to come here and watch you. I am here to make a difference, and if any of you are interested, you may even learn a few things. Now, I left very early this morning, so it might be a good idea to show me some traditional Scottish hospitality and offer me a nice cup of coffee.'

* * *

'According to Herr Schiltz's weekend itinerary, the guests – upon arrival – will be piped up the long driveway to enjoy welcome drinks in the library. Tonight is to be an informal gathering with a buffet supper laid out in the Grand Hall on the ground floor. The terrace doors will be open as it's forecast to be a beautiful weekend.' Julie's accent is a soft burr, and she leads me into the Grand Hall. 'I'll show you.'

I contemplate the large mahogany panelled walls on the far side of the room and stone-walled room to my right with its massive fireplace that would once have roasted venison or a whole lamb on a spit.

'This is incredible,' I say.

'I felt the same when I came here a few weeks ago,' she whispers. 'Isn't it beautiful?'

Above us, around the inner walls, is an interior corridor decorated with numerous tapestries, family portraits, and old painted landscapes in gilt frames.

'Fortunately, Mrs Long has hired some additional local staff. They're helping; carrying tables and chairs and organising plates and cutlery.'

I watch Mrs Long bustle around the hired staff as she issues instructions.

'She likes to oversee the flower arrangements, tablecloths and that sort of thing.'

'Are you from Aberdeen?' I ask.

'I'm from Edinburgh originally, but I'm thinking of moving here.'

Mrs Long sees us and makes her way over to stand beside me.

'The main staircase.' She points to the nearside wall. 'Will take you upstairs to the library and small hall and then the battlements. The guests can access their bedrooms along the inner corridor, or there's a separate entrance in each corner of the Grand Hall.' She points up at the inner corridor and then at three solid wooden doorways at the end of the hall. 'The north tower, south tower and east tower.'

'I hope I can explore the castle later,' I say.

'There won't be time,' Mrs Long replies.

I look at Julie, but she turns quickly away without meeting my gaze.

Mrs Long continues, 'The guests will be dining inside on both nights. Presumably, Herr Schiltz dislikes eating al fresco, and so tonight is a buffet, and we'll set the table up along the far wall. Tomorrow for the formal dinner they shall be inside sitting down at the main table in the centre of the room for Mrs Schiltz's birthday celebration. The staff will move the table after the breakfast buffet in the morning back to the centre of the room.'

'The flowers smell magnificent,' I say admiring a large arrangement of stocks, roses and lilies.

Mrs Long looks at her watch. 'Where's Mac?' She walks back to the kitchen, and Julie and I follow her. 'Where's Mac?' she calls.

Dan walks past, carrying two stacked up chairs. 'They want extra chairs,' he explains. 'At least if they dine at the big table tomorrow it'll save all the hassle of carrying these in and out.'

'Yeah, and keep all the flies away,' Julie says.

Dan gives me a lopsided grin. 'It's normally my job to stand beside the buffet table, swatting them away from the food, and I'm supposed to pretend I'm doing something else.'

'Dan, stop prattling and do something useful. Get out the linen tablecloths, as I've shown you before. You know where they are, go on.' Mrs Long pulls up the sleeves of her white tunic and back in the kitchen, Julie begins to roll vegetables into round balls.

'I'll taste those before you finish the seasoning,' I say to her, and she smiles back.

I nip to the bathroom, and I pull out my white tunic and wrap a colourful blue and white bandana around my hair. Afterwards, I consult my notes and then take myself off to the storerooms to check the ingredients against what I'd ordered.

I work my way through the storerooms, pantry and fridges, and it must be an hour later when I return to the kitchen with the fresh lamb. I pull out my own set of Japanese knives in a brown leather roll and a canvas storage case. The collection includes paring, utility, small and large santoku, small and large chef's, bread and carving knife with canvas storage case.

'Are they authentic?' Dan asks.

I smile, pleased he's impressed. They were a gift from Tina after I left the army and began my new career. I select the meat knife.

'Mrs Long has gone for a break,' he explains, standing beside me and I'm conscious of his nervous energy as he moves from one foot to the other.

'I watched you on *Masterchef*, Ronda. Didn't you train with Monica Galetti?'

'That was a while ago,' I reply, not looking at him but concentrating on slicing the lamb into cubes.

He watches me while I prepare the marinade: garlic cloves, fresh rosemary, Dijon mustard, pepper and fresh lemon juice.

'Do you want to put the lamb on skewers for me?' I ask him.

'Are you a chef all the time now?'

'Yes, I'm freelance.'

'Don't you want your own restaurant?' He works carefully and diligently.

'I'd love to, but it takes money.'

I straighten my shoulders and with the sharp knife in my hands, I think of James and the money I'd saved. I'd found the perfect location, on the south coast of England, a small restaurant that I knew would work but then …

Julie interrupts my thoughts, saying, 'Ronda, have you met Hugo, the sommelier?'

'Hello, Ronda.' I turn at the sound of my name and find myself staring into the eyes of a lovely well dressed, dark-haired man.

'Hello, Hugo.' I smile. 'Sorry, my hands are filled with spicy marinade.'

'That's alright. It's good to meet you, Ronda. Thank you for sending me the menus by email. It's good to get a heads up on what they're eating. Herr Schiltz is very particular about his wine choice.'

'Really? Is he a wine expert?' I ask, trying not to keep smiling at him like a stupid teenager.

'An expert? Probably not but he knows what wines he likes, that's for sure. So, I have to be quite careful.' Hugo grins; his hair is gelled into a quiff and shaved at the back of his neck. His sallow skin adds to his continental air and exotic charm.

'Are you French?'

'I was born in Bordeaux, but I was brought up in Paris.'

My body tenses. That's where James proposed last Christmas.

Hugo looks around the kitchen. 'Where are all the glasses, Dan?'

The two men disappear, and I'm alone with Julie who continues to work in silence, chopping and slicing. She doesn't look up and, for the first time, I allow myself to remember James.

My ex – until six months ago – had been charming, funny, witty, and often irreverent. He was intelligent and smart, but I found out he'd used me, and my savings, to invest in his business – online gaming, he'd called it. He'd convinced me that it was the new craze, the latest fad and it's where all the big investors were putting their money. And, like an idiot, I'd believed him. I couldn't think why a man as good-looking as James would actually want me – an ex-military officer. But James had made me feel special. He'd complimented me, paid me attention, listened to me and, of course, he loved me to cook for him. I felt better about myself, and my confidence grew. The shackles of my past, the conflict war zones, and the insults from my dead father began to recede, and I began to emerge as a new butterfly in the world; happy, colourful and free. By the time James proposed last Christmas and planned our wedding in February – I was ready for our new future together. I was prepared to be a wife and hopefully, one day, a mother.

I glance over at Julie, but she doesn't look up. She can't see the turmoil churning inside me, and I'm reminded again of how I was, how I used to be.

I hadn't looked up – not once.

I didn't notice when James returned with flight tickets to Paris, or even after he'd bought our wedding rings and outfits on my credit card. I hadn't taken much notice after I'd given him my savings when he'd told me figures for his online gaming company were growing, and he was making money, because I'd trusted him. He was my future husband. I didn't look up until our wedding day. That's when I'd waited with Tina in the registry office. February 14th, and we waited, and we waited, and James had never appeared.

'Are you alright?' Julie's quiet burr interrupts my thought. 'Is it the onions? They are strong.'

'I'm fine. Thank you.' I wipe my eyes with the back of my wrist and then onto my apron. 'It's the spices. It happens sometimes.'

Julie nods in understanding, but as I turn and wash my hands, I can still feel her thoughtful gaze on me. My mood turns darker, and suddenly I'm filled with anger. I started kickboxing classes to tone my body, but it was also a vent for my emotions. I pick up my large santoku and bring it down unnecessarily heavily on a thick gourd and it splits apart. I need to exercise before I do some serious damage to someone.

Chapter 4

'We are only falsehood, duplicity, contradiction; we both conceal and disguise ourselves from ourselves.'
Blaise Pascal

An hour before the guests arrive, I manage to escape from the kitchen. It's quiet. The prep work is finished, and the Grand Hall is prepared for the evening buffet. The staff seem to have drifted away, and I know Julie is in the garden, smoking and talking to Mac. Hugo says the family will meet in the library for pre-dinner drinks.

I intend to explore the castle – I'm Inspector Joachin García Abascal's eyes and ears and besides, I'm curious to see the castle.

I spend a few minutes in the Grand Hall then I climb the beautiful stone staircase, admiring the thick stone walls. It's a respite from the hot kitchen, and I take my time, admiring the old tapestries hanging along the corridor; dramatic battle scenes, aged and worn. The golden-framed oil paintings are of serious-looking men in traditional tartan kilts and dark jackets. In some, a regal, thin-faced man poses with recent trophies; deer, rabbits, grouse.

I glance into the library – a traditionally decorated room

in hues of yellow, orange and tamarind, worn sofas, upright padded chairs, comfortable armchairs, placed around a long coffee table adorned with magazines and trinkets. The far wall is lined with old, dusty books, and I smile. It's like a scene from a film. Did they design it deliberately this way? It's a chicken and egg scenario. Which came first? The film or the original library?

In the corner, drinks have been prepared. Various shaped polished glasses sparkle in the late afternoon sunlight, bottles of spirits, an ice bucket, and six bottles of champagne are chilling in a silver bowl. The room holds no further interest for me, and I wonder how I should report all this to Inspector Joachin.

Up another narrower flight of stairs is the small hall. It has a high barrel-vaulted ceiling, stained glass windows along the far wall and a large oval window at the far end where I stand for a while marvelling at the natural light shining through three large, south-facing stained-glass windows and the patterns the colours make on the floor.

It's simply breathtaking.

'Hello, you're Ronda – the chef, aren't you? I'm Paula.'

'Hello, I was having a cheeky wander around. It's so beautiful.'

Paula – Herr Schiltz's secretary – is tall and skinny, with long blonde flowing hair to her waist. She's dressed formally in a smart cream suit.

'Sorry, we didn't actually meet up in London. It was all a bit crazy. This was all arranged last minute. It's been frantic, and I'm just making the last minute checks. I was heading down to the kitchen shortly to see you. Thank you for sending the emails – and I apologise for messing you around with some of the menus. It's sometimes hard to get everyone to agree …'

I return Paula's smile, and I notice dark circles around her anxious eyes.

'That's absolutely no problem.' I feel quite sorry for her. 'Have you organised the whole weekend?'

'Yes. I'm just wondering about the dancers and what time they will arrive. They're performing Scottish dancing before dinner.'

'How wonderful.'

'It would be if I could find them, but they won't be here until later.' She checks her notes on the clipboard in her arms and looks at the expensive watch on her wrist.

'Is it a busy itinerary?' I probe.

When she shakes her blonde head, her hair barely moves, apart from one strand which she pulls away from her eyes with a long, manicured pink nail.

'I suppose I've organised worse, well not worse, but more complicated. Like the time Herr Schiltz flew everyone to the Caribbean for his wedding, but this is …' She scratches the back of her head. 'More challenging. You see, I've been to the Caribbean, and I know my way around and what's expected but I've never been to Scotland before. It's hard to know how to go about things and sometimes people aren't very … 'Her voice trails off.

I hear footsteps behind us.

'Hello?' Hugo appears looking dashingly handsome in black trousers, black waistcoat, a white shirt and red bow-tie. 'Have you both escaped?' He grins.

'I was having a nosy,' I admit.

'And I was taking a quick break.' Paula smiles, and I wish I had her slim figure and easy swaying walk. I notice Hugo's approval as she turns on her heels and walks toward the door. We both watch her pert bottom in her tight skirt.

'We were admiring the small hall,' I say to distract him.

'Ah, yes. The small hall,' Hugo announces theatrically, casting his arms wide. 'Castle Calder dates back to 1575, and the Calder family have appeared in historical scripts since the beginning of civilisation. Cale signifies wood, and dor represents water, and as you can see from the top of the tower, from the battlements, the view represents the woods and the water. You can probably see from here too.' He looks out of the oval window.

'Ah, we have a tour guide in our midst.' I move to stand beside him. The view is stunning. The sun glistens on the rustling leaves, and the water in the river at the end of the garden shimmers invitingly on this warm August afternoon.

'But that's not everything.' Hugo smiles at me and warms to his oration as he moves back into the room. 'The name Cawdor, that you may remember from Shakespeare's *Macbeth*, is an early phonetic spelling of Calder, as pronounced in the lowlands and northeast coast of Scotland.'

I clap, and Hugo gives a bow of his head.

Paula looks puzzled.

'Are you not impressed?' I ask Paula.

'I'm worried the dancers won't turn up. I'd better go and investigate.'

'Before you go,' Hugo announces grandly. 'You might like to tell your guests that Calder is a very ancient Morayshire, Scottish family.'

'Right! Thank you. I will.' Paula hurries off with her clipboard under her arm.

'Was it something I said?' Hugo asks in mock despair.

'Probably, are you like this with all the women?'

'You guessed. My secret is out.'

'Is that why you turned to wine and became a sommelier?' I giggle.

'Of course, but that—' he taps the side of his nose '—is my secret. Now, tell me, Ronda. Are you exploring too?'

I check my watch.

'I was, but I fear my time has run out. Cinderella must return to the kitchen.'

Hugo laughs. 'But I haven't told you about the castle's private parties yet, or the team building facilities, or the product sales launches, or even concerts that they hold here in the grounds.'

'Er, no, you haven't. Sorry, your time is up.'

Hugo looks crestfallen. 'But what about the perfect wedding and the fireworks that dazzle the skies, and the floodlights that illuminate the perfect Scottish castle – the ultimate fairy-tale and romantic venue for marriage.'

'Um, no, sorry. It's not doing anything for me.'

He steps closer and whispers, 'What about the secret passageways?'

I hesitate, wondering if he's joking and I sigh dramatically.' Must dash, Hugo! Toodle pip!' I say reluctantly, enjoying the silly banter.

Hugo waves from where he's moved to stand and look out of the window. 'Farewell, princess, and be sure not to leave your golden slipper on the staircase.'

'I'll be careful.'

'Good. Or one of the guests may trip over and fall, and will want to sue you …'

I can hear Hugo laughing as I descend the stone staircase, and I think what I could report back to Inspector Joachin.

He's given me a unique mobile phone so that I can send him regular messages and updates about the people invited for the weekend. He said I should tell him everything, and no detail would be too small. Will I tell him it's a castle with secrets and the potential to be sinister? How I will describe Hugo and Paula? But when I reach the bottom step, Mrs Long is standing with her arms folded waiting for me. She is scowling. 'I wondered where you'd gone. Those rooms up there are out of bounds.'

* * *

I'm finishing the garlic and olive oil dressing for the grilled Scottish langoustines when there's a noise outside, and a commotion in the doorway.

'They're here,' Mac announces. He's changed into a three-piece tartan suit and a white shirt. His eyes are glowing excitedly, and it looks as if he's trimmed his beard. 'Best be ready, Mrs Long. The chauffeur drove up from London and picked Herr Schiltz up from the airport but they're all walking up the drive together.'

Mrs Long rips off her apron, and I notice that she's repaired her makeup and tidied her hair. She follows him out of the kitchen while I finish the last of the sponge mixture for the birthday cake.

'How many tiers?' Julie asks.

'Two or three. They haven't been specific.'

Dan leans across the worktop. 'Do you want to watch? It's quite a spectacle. John will pipe the guests up the driveway.'

'Where's Mrs Long?' Julie asks.

'She always watches the guests arrive through a gap in the

bricks in the garden wall.'

'Won't they mind the kitchen staff gawping at them?' I grin.

'Follow me. We can go upstairs and spy from the window in the hallway. Come on, Ronda. Come on, Julie. Let's go!'

I follow Dan and Julie out of the kitchen and up the back staircase to the next floor where we stand outside the library, looking through the arch window down onto the long driveway.

A lone piper in red tartan pipes in the guests. The sound is hauntingly sad. He strolls up the drive and the guests follow him.

'We'd better not let them see us.' Julie stands to one side of the window.

'They can't see us from here.' Dan grins. 'I've tested it out.'

'Cheerful music.' Hugo has crept up behind us and, leaning over Dan's shoulder for a better look, I'm conscious of his fresh aftershave; spicy, lemon?

'Quite apt, looking at their cheerful faces. God, they look positively miserable, don't they?' Hugo says. 'I thought this was supposed to be a birthday weekend.'

'The small group have been dropped off by a minibus at the entrance. The driver will wait until the guests are inside and then he'll drive their bags to the main door,' Dan explains. 'Do you recognise any of them?'

'That's Herr Schiltz, leading the group,' I say. 'I met him, and the woman holding his arm, I assume, is his wife.'

She's much younger and is beautiful. It reminds me of the question asked so often of younger women with older men – what first attracted you to the billionaire …?

Hugo says, 'The two tall men at the front are his sons by his first wife, with their partners. I think the younger ones are his wife's children by her first marriage. Then there's his business partner Mike, who I have met, that's the stocky fellow in the yellow jacket with his wife …'

'Who's the tall lady?' asks Julie

'I think that's Mrs Schiltz's best friend, she's married to Mike.'

'Do you know them well?' I ask Hugo.

'As well as I'd like to know them,' he replies. 'Herr Schiltz knows what he likes and doesn't like, and you're not allowed to get it wrong. He's a hard taskmaster,' he sighs, and looks at me. 'Let's hope you don't mess up on the menus.'

I grin. 'I won't.'

'You don't look too fazed?'

'I'm not.'

He smiles. 'Tell me that after he reduces you to tears and you run back to the kitchen sobbing.'

'I won't.'

'I've seen him treat grown men with contempt and he's left them quivering because they served his soup cold.'

'It won't happen to me.' I walk away from the window. I've seen enough of the guests and I still have lots to do.

'You're very confident about your cooking,' Hugo calls after me.

'I am,' I lie.

'Cocky!' Hugo laughs aloud.

'That's me,' I sing, and when I glance back at him, Dan and Julie are watching our exchange in bewilderment. I call out, 'Just make sure you don't serve them any crap wine or it could ruin his palate for the whole weekend and wreck my gourmet feast.'

* * *

Although I'm joking with Hugo, inside I'm trembling. Fortunately, Julie is a great help, and Dan's good humour has helped me through the day, but now the guests are here and I'm feeling overwhelmed.

Hugo is right.

What if it's a disaster and Herr Schiltz isn't happy?

The kitchen is empty. I place the sponge mixture for the birthday cake in the trays, pouring the cake batter carefully. I hear the sound of a van at the back door as the dance troupe arrive. It skids on the gravel and parks outside the back door. It's evident that they have been here on many occasions and the four females and four males, and the two pipers dressed in traditional Scottish attire, breeze into the castle via the kitchen in a whirlwind of laughter, good humour and banter.

Mrs Long ushers them through the kitchen and upstairs to the small hall. Behind them, a solid, well-muscled, bareheaded man walks in carrying an overnight bag. He nods but doesn't smile.

'I'm Jim.'

'Hello, Jim,' Julie answers cheerfully and she points him in the direction of the bedrooms through the Grand Hall. After he's gone she says to me, 'You wouldn't want to mess with him, would you?'

I shake my head. I've met men like him in the army. He's a thug.

Half an hour later, Julie is finishing the canapés, and the waiting staff are in the corner of the kitchen where Hugo is instructing them on the formalities of the evening.

While the guests are busy upstairs with the entertainment, I decide it's a good time to have a final look at the buffet display. Rather than disturb Hugo's lecture, I walk out of the back door and around the castle, across the garden to where the terrace doors of the Grand Hall are open. Upstairs, from the small gallery, I hear the bagpipes followed by clapping and then the soft tapping of feet on the wooden floor. Occasionally there's a whoop of joy, and the guests clap louder. Whoop, whoop, and a burst of applause.

The Grand Hall is empty, and I check the table is ready for the plates of food. I imagine the layout as I described it earlier to Dan, who was supervising the extra waiting staff. I move a few things on the table around, the plates nearer to the cutlery, and the seasoning and sauces at the far end. Small things, but simple to make buffets easier. When I'm finished I exit the same way and bump straight into Mac. He's carrying a rifle.

'My goodness, you gave me a fright,' I say.

'The guests are all upstairs. Are you alright?'

'I'm fine. What's that for, intruders?'

He shakes his head thoughtfully. 'I've just shown the chauffeur upstairs to his accommodation. He was asking about the guns for tomorrow.'

'I hope you leave the safety catch on.'

He gives me a strange look. 'I'm always careful.'

'It's not you that I'm worried about.' I grin, but I'm surprised at my own words, and I'm suddenly unsettled as if this idyllic castle holds some extraordinary power over us. I watch him turn and walk away and a growing unease ripples through me. It's like a chilled breath on my cheeks and I'm suddenly filled with a sense of foreboding, similar to the feelings I experienced in the army.

Chapter 5

'Frank and explicit — that is the right line to take when you wish to conceal your own mind and to confuse the minds of others.'
Benjamin Disraeli

Grilled Scottish langoustines, epic lamb kebabs, vegetable balls, smoked salmon blinis, baked camembert, spatchcock chicken and wild rice. Soufflés, homemade ratatouille and chopped salad – it all takes time to prepare and the time flies along with a flurry of kitchen activity.

Julie is efficient but not professional, willing but not always capable, and Dan and Hugo liaise between us and the temporary waiting staff. I'm directing the staff as though I'm conducting a fine orchestra, waving my arms but also adding the finishing touches to sauces, rearranging plates of succulent roasted meats and plates of fish.

Ten guests for dinner isn't a great amount but I'm conscious of the number of other staff like Paula and Mr Schiltz's chauffeur who will eat afterwards in the kitchen. I don't take much notice of the people coming in and out of the kitchen, or the staff employed for the evening until Paula suddenly appears in the doorway.

Mrs Long reacts first. She heads forward determinedly, but

somehow Paula manages to swing past her and, circling the long central table, she's at my side.

'Herr Schiltz would like to see you.'

'Now?'

'Yes.'

'His timing's good.' I use my sarcastic voice. 'Doesn't he realise this is my busiest time?'

Paula looks apologetic and shrugs. 'He probably does but he wants to talk to you anyway.'

I wash my paring knife and dry it carefully before following Paula from the kitchen. I'm conscious of my stained white tunic and the colourful bandana that covers my short hair. I haven't had time to look at my face or makeup since this morning and I guess I must look a mess; hot and sweaty.

I follow Paula across the Grand Hall where a couple of the waiting staff, dressed in black and white uniforms, are bustling backwards and forwards, carrying dishes and plates of hors d'oeuvres toward the library. Hugo hurries past carrying several chilled bottles of expensive Krug champagne and he winks.

Instead of taking me to the library, as I expect her to do, Paula heads to the far tower and we begin the narrow ascent of the stone staircase. We pass two closed bedroom doors on the first floor and we climb up to the second floor where I assume Herr and Frau Schiltz's bedroom is.

Paula knocks tentatively and when he calls out, she enters their bedroom speaking fluent German, before standing aside to let me pass.

Herr Schiltz is standing at the window gazing down into the garden. I know some of the guests are in the library and some, I can hear, have already ventured outside. Their riotous laughter floats up through the open window.

'They're horsing around out there in the garden, get them into the library, Paula,' Herr Schiltz says. 'I'll be down in a few minutes.'

'Yes sir.' Paula closes the door on her way out and I stand waiting just like I used to stand waiting for my father's attention.

So often, I'd been summoned to his office. He'd pretend to be busy or preoccupied as if he had some difficult task, or worry or hurdle that only he could surmount. It was as if he alone could solve the problem, and I had to watch and admire him; he wanted me to think about how he could be so talented, clever and wonderful. But it never worked. I just became resentful and snide – not characteristics I'd actively pursued – until now.

'You want to speak to me?' I prompt, my tone bordering on the insolent.

Herr Schiltz turns from the window. He's wearing a tartan green kilt and waistcoat and a navy jacket and bowtie. It seems pretentious. I bite my lip. I don't smile. But once he focuses his narrow eyes on me and I see his pencil moustache my heart flips a beat and my mouth feels suddenly dry.

'I need you to do something for me.' He stands with his index finger and thumb in the small pocket of his waistcoat.

'Okay.' I swallow hard, and I have a sense of foreboding. Whatever Herr Schiltz wants from me, I know I won't like it.

'Have you made the birthday cake yet?'

'I made the sponge this afternoon. The cake will be ready tomorrow, the day of your wife's birthday, so I'll decorate it first thing.'

'Good. Good.' He walks with long strides and as he draws up

in front of me, he pulls something from his waistcoat pocket. 'I want you to put this inside the cake for me.'

He holds out the biggest diamond I have ever seen. It's a massive rock – and it's blue.

'It's a very expensive ring,' he says quietly twisting it between his fingers. 'A blue diamond, six carats.'

'It's stunning.'

'There are two smaller pink diamonds on the side, see? The band is made of platinum.'

'It's … it's beautiful.'

He pulls the ring away from me. 'Of course, it's beautiful – and extremely valuable. If I told you how much, you'd probably faint. I want it to be a surprise for my wife. No one must know about it.'

'I won't say a word.'

He turns and faces me. 'I know you won't. It would be more than this job is ever worth to you. I'd destroy your reputation.'

I stare at him. I don't reply that my reputation has been greatly embellished. I don't tell him that my relationship with royalty and celebrities has been exaggerated to boost my sagging confidence. I don't tell him I'm bankrupt and that there's nothing to destroy. I don't tell him that I'm prepared to walk away right now and tell him to shove his ring where the sun doesn't shine. I refuse to look away.

'I want you to put this inside the cake as a surprise.'

'It might get …' I'm trying to think of the right word. How can you say a blue diamond probably worth a couple of million pounds will get dirty? Is that what he wants? The ring filled with bits of sponge?

He grins but he looks more like a predatory wolf than a married man. 'It'll be fun. She won't expect it.'

'I'm sure it will be a lovely surprise.'

'I must be able to cut that piece for my wife. Can you do that?'

'Of course. I can mark it.'

I'm curious about Frau Schiltz and I wonder what her reaction will be when she is presented with a slice of cake and this ridiculously expensive blue diamond ring.

'I'll make sure you have the ring early in the morning. I'll bring it to you in the kitchen. But no one, absolutely no one must know.'

'Your secret is safe with me.'

'Let's put it like this, Ronda.' He moves closer to me and there's whisky on his breath. 'You're the only one that knows about this, so if anything happens to it I'll know where to come.'

I blink. A sudden rush of tears runs to my eyes. 'I wouldn't—'

'You'd be a very stupid woman,' he spits. 'If you thought of double-crossing me.'

I'm still shaking my head in denial.

'Go, now. I'll see you in the kitchen at six in the morning but before that, come to the library in thirty minutes, I want them all to see you.'

I nod my head subserviently as I leave, cursing myself, but feeling pathetically relieved to be away from him. I stomp blindly down the deep stone spiral staircase, drying my eyes on the back of my hand but I'm distracted by the sound of loud voices from behind the bedroom door on the floor below.

An argument?

I pause and hold my breath.

'I'm not putting up with it – that's FINAL!'

There's scuffling and the shouting stops, then suddenly, the second bedroom door opens and a thick, heavy figure fills the light. Jim is standing in the doorway. He's taken off his jacket and under his shoulder is a holster and a pistol.

I continue quickly, running, holding the rope bannister descending the stairs rapidly. The only satisfaction I have, in this whole silly place, is to think that Herr Schiltz's secret isn't safe with me. Not at all. I have every intention of sharing it with someone far nicer and much worthier than Herr bloody Schiltz.

Chapter 6

Half an hour later, I'm dressed in my dirty whites, but I remove my bandana and wear my best smile when I'm ushered into the library by the unsmiling Paula. Again, she stands aside at the door to let me pass as if she's only allowed to proceed into the first square metre of the room. Standing in the doorway and seeing the sea of unknown faces, I mutter as I pass her, 'Once more unto the breach…'

I hear her giggle before she bows out of the room.

I'm the focus of attention for everyone in the room, their conversation dies on their lips and their curious eyes seem to feast upon me.

Frau Schiltz, the woman who had held her husband's arm walking up the long drive, approaches me and holds out a hand. She greets me in a southern British accent.

'Hello, Ronda. I'm Louisa, thank you so much for cooking for us this weekend. We're really looking forward to sampling your recipes.'

She's a slim, fair-haired elegant lady who's had Botox.

She looks far younger than the fifty years she'll celebrate tomorrow, and unfortunately, her youthfulness only makes her husband look much older.

'It's my pleasure.'

A tall, angular faced, but handsome woman at her side is quick to shake my hand. 'I'm Fran, Lou's best friend. I saw you win *Masterchef* on television. It's my favourite programme.'

'If only you'd learn something from it!' a short man in a beige suit quips.

'I must have the only wife in the world that can't make toast without burning it.'

'Stop complaining, Mike.' Louisa laughs good-naturedly. 'You can't have everything in this life. The best boss in the world *and* the best wife!'

'I'm not his boss,' Herr Schiltz frowns irritably. 'Mike is my business partner.'

'Oh yes, silly me, you know how I don't understand these things very well.'

I hide a smile. By her teasing tone, I guess she's said that deliberately. Louisa Schiltz is not to be underestimated and judging from her husband's business partner's sullen face, she knows which buttons to press.

'You understand very well, Mum. You know exactly. You've been friends with Fran and Mike for how long?'

A skinny man, younger than me in his late twenties, drains his glass of champagne and wanders over. 'I think you do it deliberately.' Then he whispers theatrically, 'I *know* you do.'

He wears Ray-Ban sunglasses that he's pushed up onto his head, and they hold back his long, dark curly hair. His face is tanned. It's an expensive tan, perfect like his manicured hands.

'Your mother and I have been friends for forty years, Jack,'

Fran says. 'It's her humour.'

'I don't think my mother has a sense of humour, does she, Freya? Does our mother make jokes?'

Freya looks up from the sofa, her mobile in her hand that is clearly the focus of her attention. She hasn't been listening to the conversation and when she sees Herr Schiltz, her stepfather, frowning she attempts to hide her phone behind her back.

Hugo is hovering in the background, moving almost invisibly, refilling glasses. Jack holds his glass out for a refill. Hugo doesn't look at me.

'Where's Gunter? Why is he always late?' Herr Schiltz covers his champagne glass, clearly not wanting a refill.

'Hi, I'm Chloe – Wilhelm's girlfriend.' A young girl with an American accent and dark eyes set too close together appears at my side. 'I've never watched *Masterchef* but Louisa and Fran have raved about you and your cooking. Is it true you've cooked for the Queen of England?'

'I've only cooked for William and Kate—'

'And Charles and Camilla,' Herr Schiltz interrupts. He clearly fell for the exaggerated credentials I presented to him.

'Wow! Are they like they are on TV?' Chloe drawls.

I smile. 'I spent most of my time in the kitchen, but they were very friendly and appreciative.'

'Did they pay you lots?' Wilhelm is Herr Schiltz's son. He has the same narrow face and wide mouth but without the pencil moustache and remains seated on the sofa while he waits for Hugo to refill his glass. He's broad-shouldered, and I can imagine women would find him attractive but he reminds me of a younger version of my father. He stares at me like I'm a child, almost as if I've done something wrong, and I know he could make me feel guilty and paranoid, so I gaze defiantly back at him, unblinking, directly into his eyes.

'Wilhelm, stop it. It's not all about the money, you know.' Chloe bashes him playfully on the arm.

We're interrupted as the door flies open. The man looks harassed and angry, and she looks positively miserable. Her eyes are red and swollen as if she's been crying.

'Sorry, we're late, Father.'

I recognise his voice and realise that this must be Gunter and his wife Roma, who have the bedroom on the floor below his father. It was his voice that I heard shouting earlier.

'Are you alright, Roma?' Louisa asks.

'Hay fever,' Roma replies apologetically. 'I think it must be the flowers,' she adds to her lie.

Hugo flicks a glance in her direction, smiles, and offers them a tray. 'Would you like champagne?'

Gunter grabs a glass and moves away, leaving Roma to stand with Chloe. Mike moves away nearer to me.

'Now we're all here. We can get on with things – er, Ronda, you can go now. Go back to the kitchen,' Herr Schiltz dismisses me.

I take a step backwards, insulted by his abruptness.

Wilhelm stands up muttering. He frowns and then he asks,' What's that smell? Can you smell it? It's like, aftershave, it's like …'

He receives another blow to his arm from Chloe.

'Stop it, Wilhelm.'

He frowns.' No, I mean it. It's like …'

Fran moves toward him, and there's a heavy scent of Christian Dior.

'This castle is a maze, and we ended up on the battlements,

didn't we, Mike? The view is amazing. Has anyone else been up there yet?'

Jack nudges his sister Freya, who is trying not to look at the screen of her mobile. 'We haven't been allowed. We've already been ordered in from the garden.'

'Excuse me,' I say. 'I have a meal to finish. I do hope you enjoy it.' I leave the library and exhale deeply in the corridor, just as Paula steps out of the shadows.

'How did it go?' she whispers.

'I feel as though I survived a mauling in the Colosseum.'

She giggles but says seriously, 'That's nothing. Wait until later and after they've all had a few drinks.'

'Oh, joy. Well, I'll be in bed way before all of that kicks off.'

I head toward the stairs, but I pause to look back just as Paula enters the library. I see a snapshot of the family gathering but it doesn't look like a happy occasion. There are certainly undercurrents of resentment, anger, and I wonder what else. How will I report this all back to Inspector Joachin?

* * *

The kitchen is hot, and we're all kept busy, so when there's a lull while they eat their desserts, I venture outside into the cooler air.

It's past nine o'clock and growing dark. I find a bench against the secluded herb garden, lean my head back against the hard brickwork and close my eyes. It's been a long day. I was at the airport at six this morning, and it seems an age ago.

It's still early enough to give Tina a ring and check on Molly, so I pull out my mobile from my pocket.

There's a sound to my left. My body stiffens. Soft footsteps, then Jim appears walking along the path. He's menacing and threatening. He ignores me and walks into the kitchen.

Tina doesn't answer her phone, so I leave a message then I sit listening to the nocturnal sounds of the garden stirring, and eventually I pull myself up from the bench and wander back into the kitchen.

Julie is sitting at the table and has a bowl of untouched pasta in front of her.

'Where is everyone?' I ask.

She shrugs. 'I went to the loo, and when I came back, Mac says Dan and the waiting staff have gone, and Mrs Long looked exhausted so I said I'd finish up.'

'I was expecting Paula to eat with us and Mac and Jim – and maybe even Hugo.'

'Paula went to her room with a sandwich, and she took one for Jim. Mac says he's been wandering around everywhere.'

'And the guests?'

Julie smiles. 'The young ones don't want to go to bed; they're still drinking.'

'Is that pasta good?'

She pulls a face. 'It looks terrible…'

'Why are you eating it then?'

'Mrs Long said she made it for the staff and I haven't eaten all day.'

I reach over and take the bowl and tip it quickly into the bin.

'Leave it to me. I'm sure I can find us something much nicer.'

I spend a few minutes rummaging around in the pantry and then the fridge and I place chopped salad, Scottish langoustines and smoked salmon on the table.

'My goodness,' Julie gasps, staring at the mouth-watering dishes. 'We shouldn't.'

I grin. 'Why not? Come on, tuck in, there's enough for us both, and I'll see if I can find us some plonk to go with it.'

I find a chilled bottle of Chablis in the fridge.

'We can't drink that,' Julie says.

'Are you driving?'

'No.'

'Good.' I pour us both a healthy measure. 'Cheers! To us. We deserve it.'

Julie grins. She looks exhausted and pale, like someone who rarely goes outside and enjoys the sunshine or good weather.

'What will Hugo say?' she asks.

'I'll tell Hugo the mice drank it.'

Julie laughs as I serve her a healthy plate of food.

'Where is Hugo?' I ask.

She shrugs. 'He's around somewhere. I've never been so spoilt,' she says, eyeing the plate of food.

'Really? It's a perk of the job, look at the size of me.'

'You're not big.'

I laugh. 'I'm solid muscle.'

'But you're not big, Ronda. You're beautiful, Rubenesque, voluptuous—'

'Careful, or I will think this plonk has gone to your head.' I grin, happy with her description of me and ask, 'Have you been working here long?'

'For a few weeks. The last girl was sick and they needed someone urgently. They had a couple of big groups and then a hen party, and after that a wedding, so they asked me back—'

'Who asked you, Mrs Long?'

'She's the housekeeper, but she doubles up as cook when no one else is around, or it's quiet, or there's a smaller group. She's actually quite nice to me.'

'Good. Do you live nearby?'

'I'm staying in the stable at the moment.'

'Ah, the luxury accommodation,' I grin. 'I'm in those salubrious lodgings too.'

She laughs. 'I've rented a cottage in the village but because Mrs Long wants us here from dawn to dusk this weekend they offered me a room here on the estate, free of charge, and it saves me travelling back and forth.'

'How lucky,' I reply, but my sarcasm is lost on her, and she eats with gusto.

I savour the langoustines and lean back in my chair, relaxing for the first time today.

'I watched you on *Masterchef*. They did a documentary after you won about you being in the army. You're a war hero.'

I can't tell her the truth, so I sip my wine.

'Was it bad in Afghanistan?' she asks.

'Yes, and Syria and Belize...'

I finish my dinner, and when I try to ask her questions about her life, she's self-deprecating.

'Me? It's just a job and a way to pay the rent.'

It's evident that she doesn't want to talk about herself, and suddenly Julie has finished her food, and she yawns loudly.

'Would you mind if I went to bed, Ronda?'

'No, you go ahead.'

'You must be exhausted too. Didn't you fly up from London this morning?'

'I don't need much sleep, besides I think I'm too excited to sleep.'

'Is everything prepped for tomorrow?'

I pick up our dirty dishes and carry them to the sink. 'Yes, don't worry. I've got a couple of things I want to finish then

I'll head off to bed as well. Sleep tight.'

'Night, Ronda. Thank you.'

'Night, Julie.'

***

I find a bottle of brandy, pour myself a generous measure and head out to the garden and to the bench I've claimed as my own. The early evening smells of herbs, and wildflowers have disappeared, and now the heady scent of Lady of the Night lingers on the soft Scottish breeze. This is a world away from the madness of London, and I lean back, resting my head on the old brick.

I'm not looking forward to sleeping on my own. I'll miss Molly. I'll miss the way she clambers up on the bed and waits patiently for me, lying with her head on her paws, as I come out of the bathroom. Then when I get into bed, she rolls on her back for her traditional tummy rub, and when I turn off the light and lie on my side, she curls into me. I usually fall asleep to her heavy sighs and soft snoring.

I imagine her at Tina's house. She'll be in her doggy bed on the floor in Tina's kitchen. No tummy rub. No soft mattress.

A male voice complains from the other side of the wall, and I strain to listen.

'Christ, it's bloody suffocating. And, on top of everything else, I've got to go bloody grouse shooting tomorrow.'

It's Wilhelm, Herr Schiltz's youngest son.

'Is it the season?' an American woman drawls – Chloe.

'Presumably.'

'Well, think of me tomorrow, I'm going with the ladies on a tour of Loch Ness to find the monster.'

'There is no monster. It's a story made up to get stupid tourists to visit the place.'

'Don't be such a spoilsport.'

'This is a nightmare, Chloe. I hate it.'

'Come on, honey. It's not that bad.'

'It is. You've no idea. I can't stand it. I can't stand *them*.'

'But they're your family.'

'They may be, but they're certainly not my friends. Mike is behaving as if I know him well, but I haven't seen him for years – since before I moved to the States. Besides, they're not family, my stepmother and her best friend are behaving as if they're on some pathetic soap opera, prancing around giggling. She's common.'

'You do worry so much, Wil. You mustn't stress it.'

'I can't be like you, Chloe. Don't you understand?'

'Of course, I do, sweetie, but it's only for a couple more months.'

'It can't come quickly enough.'

I sit still, hardly daring to breathe.

'Jack's drunk. He's an idiot.'

'He's young, and he is family. He's your brother.'

'He's my stepbrother.' William corrects her. 'And I can't stand him. He's lazy, spoilt and he's a drunken idiot.'

'Freya is sweet.'

'She's like her mother. She's a replica of Louisa – she pretends she's funny and easy-going, but she's a manipulative whore.'

'Wil, stop it. Stop being nasty.'

'What? It's the truth—'

'It's not for much longer. Come here and hold me, it's turned chilly out here.'

'How can I survive working with him?'

'The time will fly past. Come here.' There's a hint of ridicule in her voice. 'Umm, you're lovely and warm. Just remember, in a few months, you can tell them all what to do with the company.'

'That will be worth celebrating. I told you it would be worth marrying me, didn't I?'

'I'd marry you anyway, Wil – with or without the inheritance.'

'Yeah, well, I don't know how Gunter puts up with him.'

'Gunter is a different man to you. I can never fathom him out, but he'd had a row with poor Roma. She looked positively miserable. Umm, that's nice,' she murmurs. 'I've never known two brothers to be such opposites. That's probably why Gunter stayed in London, and why you came to America.'

'America – I love it. New York suits me, my darling. You know that. I wouldn't want to live anywhere else.'

'I know, sweetie.'

Their voices become a whisper, and I hear a soft moan, and suddenly I'm uncomfortable sitting listening to the sounds of their romance in the dark. It's like I'm a voyeur, and this is how I get my kicks, but I don't move. I'm rooted to the spot, but then, just as I'm deciding what to do, Wilhelm whispers, 'Come on, let's go upstairs and make the most of that four-poster bed.'

Chloe giggles seductively. 'I thought you'd never ask.'

After they've gone I sigh with relief, quietly reflecting on their conversation, mimicking Chloe's words softly and sarcastically.

'Oh, Wil, I thought you'd never ask. Oh, Wil, take me upstairs and shag me senseless.'

'Pardon?' Mac steps out of the stone arch doorway and into

the light. 'Are you speaking to me?'

* * *

I'm smothering a giggle when Mac says, 'Have you seen the front of the castle all lit up?'

I shake my head.

'It's beautiful,' he insists. 'Leave that glass and bottle there. I'll take it inside later. We'll go this way by the south wall. There's a scenic view of the woods and the river in the day. The view is spectacular.'

I walk companionably beside Mac along the path and when the clouds part, the silvery moon shines above us lighting the pathway.

'It's a full moon tomorrow,' he says, squinting up at the sky. 'Good weather is forecast for the shooting.'

'Are you taking them?'

'Yes, of course.'

'Do you double up as night watchman too?'

He rubs his head and doesn't reply.

'Do things get a bit rowdy?' I ask.

'Sometimes, with promotional or corporate events, you know, when too much alcohol is consumed. Weddings are normally alright apart from the occasional bridesmaid vomiting in the toilet—'

'Lovely! And this group?'

'They're a bit strange. Aloof. Spoilt and rich. There's an odd mix.'

'In what way?'

He shrugs. 'They don't seem to want to be here.'

'I thought that too. It's a bit strange to *have* to be here to celebrate a birthday. You'd have thought they'd want to. I'd have thought they would be happy to hang out here, of all places.'

'That's family, I guess. They're not always your friends or the people you want to hang out with.' His voice takes on a bitter tone, and I remember he's recently-separated.

'They don't seem to like each other much,' I probe, in part for my report to Inspector Joachin but also because I'm curious.

'You're right. Herr Schiltz's business partner, Mike, has already told me not to pair him up with one of the guests tomorrow at the grouse hunt, so I'll have to rearrange things in the morning.'

'Really? Who's that he doesn't want to be paired with – Wilhelm?' I say.

Mac stops and looks at me in surprise. 'How did you know that?'

'I took a guess.'

'Do you know why?

I shake my head. I'd already shown off. Inspector Joachin wanted me to be his eyes and ears, not his mouth-almighty. I have to be more cautious.

Mac is distracted, and he takes my arm.

'Look, there. See the castle?'

I turn around to see Castle Calder illuminated in red lights, the stone walls glowing like hot coals and the peaked silver château turrets reflecting the glowing moon. A fairy-tale castle; what a perfect place to spend a birthday, unless of course, you're with the wrong people.

'It's beautiful,' I whisper.

We stand companionably then I say, 'There's someone up on the casement, up there. Look on the battlements.'

Mac squints into the distance. 'Yes, you're right.'

'Who is it?'

'Jim, the chauffeur.'

'He looks more like a bodyguard,' I reply. 'I wouldn't want to get in a fight with him.

'Very wise, Ronda. He's a very dangerous man. He also carries a gun.'

* * *

I close the door quietly and turn on my bedside lamp, conscious that the walls are thin and my neighbours will hear me moving around. I pull out my mobile and check my messages. There's one from Tina with a photo of Molly.

Sorry, we missed you. out running. missing you. Woof woof, lick, lick and goodnight.

I smile then I rummage in my weekend bag and find the particular mobile the inspector gave me.

A green flag tells me I have a message.

Read this text then delete it.

I prop up the pillows and make myself comfortable.

Ronda, if you have any news, please send a message. It doesn't matter how unimportant you think it might be or how late it is.

I begin to type.

Mr Schiltz is giving me a valuable blue diamond ring to hide in Mrs S. birthday cake at 6 am. Wilhelm, younger son, isn't happy to wait to get his inheritance? He doesn't like his family! Gunter and his wife have been arguing. Jim, the chauffeur/bodyguard, wears a Smith & Wesson.

I gaze at the ceiling for inspiration.

I've been in the kitchen with the staff. Ronda.

I sigh and toss the phone on the bed, too tired for drama. I have a quick shower, dry my hair and brush my teeth. It's after I've pulled on my cotton pyjamas and I'm sitting in bed that a message comes back.

Thank you, Ronda. This is a big help. I need to ask a favour of you. Is there any way that you can get into Herr S. bedroom? See if there are any documents?

I gaze at the ceiling, thinking of Jim and his gun when another message pings through.

BTW, can you get a photo of the ring?

I type back.

I'll try, R.

I clear the messages and switch off the phone and place it between my underwear, at the bottom of my weekend bag. I turn off the light and lay my head on the pillow.

I miss Molly's happy sigh, her wheezing and soft snores.

Inspector Joachin. Is he here in Scotland?

Chapter 7

'Look wise, say nothing, and grunt. Speech was given to conceal thought.'
William Osler

It's a bright and sunny morning, and I can feel the warmth of the sun on my back as I lock the door of my room. I'm dressed in clean whites, and today, I've put a navy, gold, orange and green bandana around my head.

'Morning!'

Startled, I turn quickly.

Hugo is wearing black shorts and a jogging vest. He's panting while trying to smile at the same time.

'You're up early,' I say.

'I try and do 5k first thing.'

'Is that all?'

He grins and begins breathing more regularly with his hands on his hips. Then he checks his watch. 'I set off at five-fifteen.'

'Really, you had a lie-in? I was up much earlier.'

'Ha ha, Ronda.'

'See you later.' I wave.

'You're starting in the kitchen early,' he calls.

'It's the normal time,' I say, with a hint of mockery in my

voice. 'I went jogging at four-thirty – sorry I missed you.'

'Yeah, yeah, yeah.'

I don't try to convince him. I know how to maintain the necessary fitness level for my cardio kickboxing, and there's a strong focus on my core. It also improves my flexibility, balance and coordination, as well as helping my reflexes. I try to work out five days a week for sixty minutes, even if I have to get up early. I need this discipline, but more importantly, it also helps me cope with my night-time demons; my nightmares about bankruptcy, serving a disastrous meal and my feelings of inferiority. Last night had been no exception.

* * *

I've balanced three sponge cakes on top of each other, mixed the icing fondant and I'm rolling it out when Herr Schiltz arrives in the kitchen wearing a navy dressing gown and maroon slippers. His moustache looks trim, and he's shaved.

'Good morning.' I force myself to smile.

He ignores me and walks around the kitchen to stand beside me. His breath smells of toothpaste. 'What's that?'

'The fondant – icing.'

'Green?'

'You wanted a golf-themed cake, didn't you?'

'Yes.'

'This will be a putting green with a hole and a flag with the number five on one side and zero on the other. I will make two figures, one of your wife and one of you, and golf clubs, and – if it works out – a golf buggy.'

'Where will we put this?' he whispers, 'the ring?'

'Wherever you like. I can cut a tiny hole and then mark the

spot with a toothpick, and when I place the fondant over the cake there will be a tiny, tiny hole and we will know the exact location.'

'Can you put something there to mark the spot?'

'Like a golf ball?'

'That would be perfect. Then I would know which piece to cut for Louisa.'

'No problem.'

I reach over, wipe my hands on my apron, and pick up my Japanese knife. I point to the top of the cake.

'Here?'

He nods.

'Do you have it?' I ask.

As I dip my knife into the soft sponge, he pulls the glistening blue diamond from his pocket. I want to whistle at its beauty, let alone the probable cost but I refrain from any silliness as I carefully gouge out a small hole. I take the ring from him, and for a few seconds, it's mine. I place it gently and neatly inside and then pack a small amount of sponge into the middle of the ring where Louisa's finger will go. It looks almost perfect. I place a toothpick in the centre of the hole inside the ring, so it stands out, marking the spot.

'Now what?' he asks.

'This.'

Herr Schiltz's breath increases in short rapid gasps as I take the rolled-out green fondant and place it carefully over the entire three layers of cake. I ease it over the toothpick, and it pricks easily through the fondant and without tearing. I leave a generous measure to tuck around and into the sides. It takes several minutes for me to cover the cake and then I stand back and look at my work.

'All done.'

He leans forward to inspect my work.

'No one would know,' I add.

'Apart from the toothpick,' he says.

I pick up a small piece of white icing and using my little knife; I sculpture dimples into the golf ball.

'There.' I hold it out to him. 'Would you like to do the honours?'

He glances at me then takes the golf ball made of icing and, removing the toothpick with his left hand, he places the golf ball over the minuscule hole left by the toothpick. Then he glares at me and strokes his moustache thoughtfully. 'Only you and I know about this. Remember that, Ronda.'

'I could never forget it.'

He picks up the small knife I used for gouging out the sponge and holds it between us, the blade pointing at me.

'Many people, cleverer than you, have tried to double-cross me but they never win.'

He raises the knife to my chest. I lick my lips, wishing my heart wasn't thumping so hard that I might faint.

'If this all goes according to plan, Ronda, then there's a substantial bonus for you – that's if my wife is happy—'

'Hello!'

We both turn at the sound of a voice. Hugo is standing at the kitchen door. His smile fades when he sees the knife, and he scowls.

'Herr Schiltz was just looking for some fruit juice for his wife.'

I turn toward the fridge as Herr Schiltz places the knife back on the table. He checks his dressing gown is tied, and he takes the glass from my hand without saying a word.

'Is everything alright?' Hugo asks after he's gone.

'Fine.' I turn my attention to the cake, but Hugo wants an answer.

'Was he threatening you?'

'No, don't be silly.' I grin. He looks doubtful. 'Okay, okay, so he did.'

I pick up the knife, the way Herr Schiltz had done, and I turn it on Hugo and say in a silly deep voice, 'Give me some juice, now, bitch!'

* * *

I continue decorating the cake, rolling and sculpting coloured fondant icing and by the time I've finished, the kitchen staff begin to arrive. They greet me with *oohs*, and *ahhhs*, and comments like, *Isn't that amazing. You're so talented, Ronda* and, *I wish I could make something like that.*

Only haughty Mrs Long sniffs silently. She busies around me, bossing the staff, getting them organised for the breakfast preparations which I will supervise.

When it's finished, I carry it through to the pantry where I know it's safe and cool. When I return to the kitchen, Jim is standing in the doorway. He's a tough-looking, broad-shouldered thug. He's squeezed into a tan-coloured jacket, and his thighs are so massive that when he sits down at the long table, his legs are spread apart.

As I prepare breakfast for the guests, Mrs Long fusses around him, and it's not long before she has served him a cooked breakfast. All the time I work, I'm conscious of him watching us all and listening. I wonder if he's aware of the hidden ring in the pantry and if he's been entrusted with guarding it all day.

'Are you going grouse hunting or to Loch Ness?' I ask him.

He stares at me before answering gruffly, 'I might stay here if Herr Schiltz doesn't go out.'

Julie intervenes. 'More toast, Jim?'

'No.'

'More bacon?'

'No. I've had enough.' He stands up, without a word of thanks. He adjusts his trouser belt and swaggers from the kitchen. Mrs Long tuts and mutters something under her breath as she picks up his empty plate. She thrusts it at Dan.

'Here,' she says. 'Clear this up.'

'Thank you, Mrs Long.' Dan shares a complicit smile with Julie, and she grins back.

'Let's just be thankful we're not married to him,' I whisper, and she giggles.

The rest of the breakfast is easy. There's a buffet laid out in the grand dining hall on the ground floor. Hugo takes the individual guests' orders for a variety of cooked breakfasts including eggs, sausages, bacon, hash browns, tomatoes and beans plus copious amounts of toast and preserves.

I prepare smoked haddock, cooked rice, eggs, parsley, and add a sprinkle of curry powder, a knob of butter and cream to make a typical Scottish kedgeree. I'm conscious of Mrs Long watching over my shoulder, waiting for me to make a mistake making one of her national, and popular, breakfast dishes. I'm meticulous about the presentation, and I call the waiting staff to carry the plates through.

Mrs Long is happy to watch, which leaves me free to finish off the picnics that the two groups are taking. I reach for the basket hampers and look around for the plates and cutlery.

'Right, everyone is happily eating breakfast, and the Glorious Twelfth is upon us,' Dan cries cheerily.

He watches me organise the picnic hampers while he explains, 'It's the beginning of the six-week hunting season when the tourists flock to our moors to shoot the grouse. How delightful ...'

'You don't approve?' I ask, concentrating on the picnic food, removing a stilton and cheddar cheese, dried tomato and basil flan from the oven that I'd made earlier.

'I don't think it's necessary to kill.'

'Well, it is.' Mac slurps his coffee in the corner of the kitchen. He's accepted a bacon roll from Mrs Long, and he eats hungrily, standing up while pretending not to look at Julie.

Mrs Long reaches for her mobile. She leaves the kitchen by the back door.

Dan shakes his head in mock bewilderment. 'So, killing grouse is obviously imperative to our national heritage – what do I know?' Dan shrugs.

He's helping me pack the wicker picnic baskets with white linen napkins and gleaming cutlery.

'They're not just grouse,' Matt sounds grumpy. 'They're iconic – the *Lagopus scoticus* – the red grouse – is our national bird—'

'Ah, that explains it all then.' Dan shakes his head in annoyance and replies sarcastically, 'It's our national bird, so let's shoot them all—'

'It's the king of game birds, and it's unique to the UK.' Mac's tone is terse.

Dan stares at him. He's busy washing pans and stacking the dishwasher, but he calls across the room, 'Ah, that's good then.'

Mac leaves his mug on the table and stomps to the back door

where he pauses, and he turns to glare.

'Look here, Dan. It flies at speeds up to 70mph, and it can change direction, in flight, in an instant—' Mac clicks his fingers.

'I'm surprised they manage to shoot them at all if they're that fast.' Dan stands his ground, and the two men eyeball each other.

'Listen, sonny. You should be proud of your heritage.'

'I am,' Dan replies. 'I just don't believe in shooting harmless and defenceless birds.'

'Are you a vegan?'

'No.'

'Then what are you complaining about?' Mac asks.

'Will you collect the picnic hampers later?' I ask Mac, anxious to avoid a rift in the kitchen.

He nods and says gruffly, 'We're leaving at ten – it's an hour's drive to the moors, but the ladies aren't leaving until eleven.'

'That's fine,' I reply and automatically begin to work faster, conscious of the work still to do for the hampers.

Julie asks, 'Why are they grouse hunting? They could go deer stalking or pheasant shooting or even salmon fishing?'

Mac shakes his head in annoyance. 'It's not for us to question them.'

'I think anything involving shooting animals is a barbaric sport,' adds Julie, looking up from the counter where she's wiping and preparing chestnut mushrooms. 'With grouse hunting, they normally have eight or ten hunters with guns who hide in butts—'

'Butts?' I look up.

'They're like shelters, and they're made of wood or stone, and they're normally covered in heather, but then there's a team of beaters who push the birds toward the butts so the guns can shoot them.'

'It's cheating using beaters,' says Dan. 'They can't even shoot them without any help.'

I listen to their descriptions, watching Mac's face growing redder.

He replies angrily, 'It's a sport, and that's that. Don't let the guests catch you talking like this.' Mac glares at Dan.

Julie doesn't look up.

Mac continues, 'It's how we make our living, so don't forget that. They pay *your* wages.'

He pushes past Hugo, who arrives holding a few bottles of wine in his arms. He looks bemused. 'For the hampers,' he whispers.

Dan suddenly laughs aloud. 'He's shaken and stirred!' He raises his fist in mock triumph.

'What's happened?' Hugo grins and then sidles up beside me and adds cheerily, 'I'm missing a bottle of Chablis.'

'It's the mice,' I mouth silently back at him. 'You missed dinner last night; they were all over the kitchen.'

He grins. 'No worries, I have more. The guests didn't drink as much as I thought they would last night.'

'Oh, good. Perhaps the mice may like another bottle tonight.'

'Only if it's shared.' He holds my gaze, and I wonder if he's flirting.

'It was shared last night but not all the mice were at the party!'

I turn away, enjoying the banter, but wondering how I will get upstairs and into Herr Schiltz's bedroom without being seen. Will Jim be here all day, keeping guard? They're hardly likely to leave that ring in the cake unmonitored.

* * *

After the men have left for the grouse shoot, Paula and I arrive at the minibus at the same time. She comes down the front stone steps while I appear from behind the wall and the path from the kitchen.

Hugo and Mac are placing the hampers in the mini bus. Three hampers for the ladies' trip to Loch Ness.

I linger, enjoying a welcome break after breakfast and the sunshine on my face.

'Are you going with them?' I ask Paula.

'I might join them later. I've got to send some emails.'

'Did Herr Schiltz go with the men, grouse shooting?'

'Yes, but Jim drove him in his car, so he'll probably be back early.'

I pull back away from the minibus as Chloe, Wilhelm's American girlfriend and Freya, Louisa's daughter, come down the steps together.

It's quite apparent that Freya wants to look at her phone, but Chloe is insisting on telling her about the research she's done on the Loch Ness monster.

'They say it's an elephant, you know,' she drawls.

Freya stands on the step next to Paula; they're the same height, and she glances at her phone.

'If you think about it, it makes sense.' Chloe uses her arm, her hand, wrist and elbow, to explain further. 'The trunk is the head of the monster, then the head and back are partly submerged in the water, creating the illusion that the monster has a skinny head and two humps.'

Freya looks at her disdainfully. 'That must be true then, Chloe. Scotland is full of wild elephants.'

'Freya,' Louisa calls from the top step. 'Make sure you have some sun lotion, although it's cloudy you can still burn in this weather.'

Freya glances over her shoulder, ignores her mother, and asks Paula, 'Is this our minibus?'

'Yes.' Paula replies, smiling, but Freya ignores her. She steps into the bus and sits at the back.

Chloe leans toward Paula. 'She's annoyed because she wanted to go grouse shooting with Jack and the men,' she explains to Paula.

I watch the exchange knowing I should leave and go back to the kitchen, but I'm curious. I watch Louisa and her best friend Fran, who looks preoccupied, descend the steps.

Fran says, 'I've got to talk to you, Louisa.'

'Well, you can. We'll be together all day.' Louisa laughs.

'No.' She lowers her voice. 'I need to tell you something, and it's vital. Can we make time to talk privately later?'

'Yes, of course.' Louisa waves at Roma. 'At last,' she calls. 'Come on, or we'll have to go without you. We're on a tight schedule, and Friedrich wants us back by four.'

Roma looks worn and tired out as if she's been awake most of the night. She's wearing a pretty yellow dress and bright pink lipstick. She's flustered, in a hurry, breathlessly waving a floaty, floral scarf.

'Sorry I'm late, Louisa. The children insisted on Skyping this morning. They wanted to wish you a happy birthday, but I said we'd call them later.'

'Lovely.' Louisa smiles. 'But not to worry, Roma. We can speak to them later. Friedrich will love that. Everyone's on board, aren't they, Paula? We must be back in time.'

Louisa climbs on the minibus, the driver turns the engine

and Paula and I watch it drive off.

I smile. 'That was uneventful.'

Paula shrugs. 'They must be back on time. I've heard there's going to be an announcement later.'

'About what?'

Paula shrugs and sighs. 'I don't know, Ronda. I wish I did because it would make my life much easier.'

'Really?' I prompt kindly. 'It can't be easy. They've all got such different personalities.'

'Oh, Ronda, I'm treading on eggshells. Some of them hate each other, and it's a minefield of emotions. I feel as though it's all going to explode.'

'Well,' I grin. 'Let's hope it's not going to happen this weekend.'

'I wouldn't put any money on that,' Paula replies. 'Underneath it all, they're quite vile to each other.'

* * *

While there's a lull in the preparations and the kitchen staff make coffee and spend time chatting, Tina calls me. It's the perfect excuse, to take the call and I step outside into the sunshine where a blackbird is chirping happily on the fence.

'Hi, Tina. How's Molly?'

As we talk, I walk around the castle via the beautiful gardens towards the open doors on the terrace and the Grand Hall. I find a quiet spot away from the door.

'She loves being here with me. I think she loves me more than she does you now.'

'Yeah, yeah.'

'How's it going up there? Has Joachin been in touch?'

I tell her quickly about the family and Jim. I walk away from the house across the manicured lawns, staying under the shade of the chestnut trees around the edge of the grounds, I whisper, 'He's asked me to go into the Führer's bedroom.'

Tina laughs before reprimanding me.

'You were supposed to be his eyes and ears, nothing more. Take care, Ronda. It's not worth risking your reputation – or your life.'

'I'm fine.'

'Yes, but I bet that's what the first Mrs Schiltz thought.'

'What do you mean?'

'I've been doing some investigating. Mrs Schiltz was killed in her own home.'

'But they caught the guy – the gardener.'

'They thought they did, but his family say there's still mounting evidence to clear his name, even though he's dead. They're furious. They maintain one of the Schiltz's family killed her.'

'Why?'

'Well, that's the thing. Have you heard of Magnum's Transport?'

'Yes, they ship a lot of valuable artefacts between museums for exhibitions and things like that. I did some catering in an art gallery a few years ago. You know the sort of thing, if a gallery lends a collection or even one painting to another gallery in another country, then it has to be transported – very carefully – and discreetly.'

'Well, that company is owned by Herr Schiltz.'

'Really?'

'Well, presumably there was a scandal five years ago. It was all brushed under the carpet, but it was at the same time the first Mrs Schiltz – Iris Schiltz was killed.'

'Do you think Inspector Joachin knows all this?'

'Of course he does, Ronda. That's why he wants you to keep an eye on things.'

'It's difficult if you don't know what to look out for.'

'Well, be careful – and phone me tonight. It doesn't matter what time you finish work; I want to speak to you.'

'I promise I will.' I hang up.

Moving quickly, I follow the shade of the trees, then I'm on the terrace and inside the open doors and the Grand Hall. I look up to check the interior balcony, but it's empty. Instead of heading for the corner tower, I run up the sweeping staircase, two steps at a time and then head to the far corner tower. It's two floors up from here. The old wooden door creaks. I cringe and pause, and then I step softly up into the round, spiral stone staircase.

I know there are three bedrooms in each tower. Gunter and Roma's bedroom door is closed. The second bedroom door is open – Jim's room. I hear a woman singing from inside and I assume the maid is making the bed and cleaning the bathroom. I haven't much time until she comes upstairs.

I lengthen my stride and pause on the next floor, wondering if I should knock on the door to Herr Schiltz's room. As a precaution, I tap lightly. When there's no answer, I open it and step inside. One of the perks of this private accommodation is that there are no locks on the outside and only an old hook and catch on the inside, used for security reasons once someone goes to bed. It's all about trust.

I look around at the cluttered mess. The four-poster bed is unmade. Pillows, cushions, and covers are strewn on the floor, and I resist picking them up. I scour the room for a suitable place for documents. There's a small bureau positioned in the window and on top of that, several pieces of paper. I flick through them, scan reading, quickly.

For this reason, I hereby resign my position.

I gasp.

There's a voice from outside, I open the door slowly, and the narrow hallway appears silent. I close the door behind me, and it's only then that I hear the lumbering steps of a heavy man climbing the stairs, his breathing rapid. He's coming closer. His shadow is on the wall. My heart's racing, my hands are clammy, and sweat pours from my forehead.

'Jim?' a voice shouts from below, and the heavy steps below me pause. He's barely a few feet away.

'Yeah?'

Paula shouts up, 'He said his briefcase is beside the bed. He's waiting in the library.'

'Right.' Jim begins to climb the stairs again, and I back away, knowing I'll never be able to hide in Herr Schiltz's bedroom.

Chapter 8

*'Look at the means which a man employs, consider his motives,
observe his pleasures. A man simply cannot conceal himself!'*
Confucius

A hand pulls me from behind. Someone grabs my arm, and I
spin around. Hugo has a finger to his lips.

'Come on,' he whispers.

I need no more encouragement.

He pushes me ahead of him, and I'm suddenly inside a dark
and confined space, a hidden laundry cupboard. He presses
up behind me, his body close against mine, and he pulls the
door quickly back into place. His mouth is beside my ear.

'Shush, don't move.'

I'm not sure whose heart is beating the fastest. His arms
are around my waist, and the muscles of his taut body are
comforting and reassuring. After the adrenalin rush of almost
being caught, my body begins to relax and sink back against his.
The footsteps stop right outside the door. My body stiffens
again.

I hold my breath, expecting the door to be pulled open.
There's a scuffle in the master bedroom and Jim curses loudly,
then his footsteps are outside again. He must be only a few

feet from us, and I hunch my shoulders, trying to make myself invisible. When I hear Jim's heavy footsteps pounding down the stone steps again, my body relaxes.

'Right, come on, this way,' Hugo whispers. He pushes me gently out of the cupboard, and instead of going downstairs, he pulls me in the opposite direction, around the corner. Here there is a smaller, much narrower flight of stairs.

'Watch your step,' he cautions me, as I climb. 'There's a small door at the top. Push it. It's easy.'

I push, and suddenly I'm blinded by natural sunlight and fresh air. I gulp heavily, breathing deeply before I realise that we're on the battlements, hidden behind the tower with the slate roof.

'Oh my goodness,' I lean on the parapet and breathe in large quantities of air, conscious of Hugo beside me, waiting patiently.

'What happened?' he asks. 'Why were you in Herr Schiltz's bedroom?'

I regard him carefully.

'How did you know about the hidden laundry room?'

'It's where the lord of the manor could hide in case there was an attack on the castle.'

'How did you find it?' I insist.

'It's what I do.' I must look puzzled because Hugo explains, 'I've worked in so many castles, Ronda. They're my favourite places. There are always secret passageways, hidden tunnels, or sinister dungeons. I make a point of locating them all within the first two hours of my arrival.'

'You do?'

'Yes.'

'Why?'

Hugo shrugs and leans on the wall beside me, overlooking the manicured lawn and rose garden to the chestnut wood and fir trees and toward the river beyond.

'I guess it makes me feel safe. I know where I am and if there's a fire or a problem, then I can always get out.'

'Umm, that makes sense.'

'Now, what about you, Ronda? Why are you up here snooping around and not in the kitchen?'

'I got lost.'

'Nice try, Ronda but if you don't tell me the truth, I guess I'll have to report you.'

I gaze at him. I know he's serious.

'I was having a wander around. There's no law against that.'

'Look, I know you didn't want to be caught, so you must be up to something.'

'Alright, alright. I'll tell you. I'm a kleptomaniac,' I confess.

He grins. 'And, I'm anything but a fool. Level with me, Ronda, or I will take you straight down to Paula and Jim where they're meeting Herr Schiltz in the library.'

I sigh. 'Okay, but you must promise that this will stay between us and you won't tell anyone else.'

'I promise.'

'Okay, well, it's like this …'

* * *

'The thing is, Herr Schiltz is exactly like my father,' I say quietly, focusing on the horizon and enjoying the morning sun on my back. 'They even have the same old Hollywood moustache. He's arrogant, rude, obnoxious and he's obviously a narcissist. And, when I met him in London, I didn't want to take this job, but I had to. I need the money.' I hold up my hand. 'Please don't ask why. That's another story.'

The intensity of Hugo's gaze disconcerts me.

I continue, 'I always wanted to be a chef but my father insisted I went to Sandhurst. He was a bully. My mother had just died of cancer, and I was broken-hearted. I couldn't stand up to him, but after he died, I was liberated. It's as simple at that, Hugo. I began working as an apprentice in some of the top restaurants in London. I applied for *Masterchef* and began my new career. But then last week, I met Herr Schiltz and, quite honestly, I was terrified. So, I came to his room this morning, hoping to speak to him alone, to ask him if he'd like to see the birthday cake I made for his wife.'

Hugo shifts position; he folds his arms, but his eyes don't leave mine.

'I want, no – I need to get his approval so that he wouldn't humiliate me later, in front of everyone, if he didn't like it.'

'So why couldn't you tell Jim that?'

I shrug. 'Because he frightens me too, but in a different way.'

'I can understand that. Jim's no more of a chauffeur than I am. He's a bodyguard. I'm sure of it.'

I nod, and I relax, breathing more easily.

'So, why was Herr Schiltz holding a knife at you this morning in the kitchen?'

'I'm sorry you saw that.'

'Well?'

'I told you, Hugo. He's a narcissist, and he threatened me. He said that if his wife wasn't happy with the birthday cake then he would be furious.'

'But he held a knife at you.' Hugo squares his shoulders. 'That's not right, Ronda.'

'I don't want to make a fuss, Hugo. I want to get through this weekend without any incidents, get paid, and go home. But in the meantime, I don't want to be humiliated. You saw what he was like in the library with me – in front of everyone. Then I get dismissed like I'm a servant, so I want to make sure he likes the cake. I don't want to be humiliated.'

Hugo frowns. 'I don't like the man.'

'Me neither. But you must be used to him and his family, haven't you worked for them before?'

'He often employs me, through Paula, of course. He hardly ever speaks to me directly unless he's with someone he wants to impress and then he talks about the wines or champagnes as if he's an expert. Then he gets me to buy expensive wine for him …'

'Then, you know him well?'

'No, hardly at all. He's not the sort of man you will ever know.'

'And what about the others?'

Hugo tilts his head and smiles. 'Ronda, for a chef, you're asking an awful lot of questions.'

That's when we hear the roar of an engine coming up the driveway, the squeal of brakes and tyres scattering gravel in all directions. There are angry voices, a car door slams and Hugo and I move simultaneously along the turreted battlements to see the action below.

'What's going on?' I ask. 'Who is it?'

'I don't know, but we'd better get back downstairs just in case anyone is looking for us.'

* * *

We hurry across the battlements, and through the door which leads down to the small hall and the library. We slip down the back stairs, past the pantry and storeroom and dungeon entrance, toward the kitchen.

'What's happened?' asks Hugo as we enter the kitchen.

It's Dan looking through the door into the Grand Hall who replies, grinning, 'They've fallen out massively.'

'It sounds like Gunter and Jack,' Julie says.

Dan adds, 'Jack reckons Gunter tried to kill him. Wilhelm is trying to stop them from killing each other.'

'Where's Mac?' I ask, but no one seems to know.

'They haven't all come back yet.' Julie looks concerned.

'We should go out there,' says Dan.

Hugo says, 'Maybe we should go and see if we can help.'

The voices fade.

'They've gone into the garden,' Dan says.

Mrs Long pushes between us all. 'It's not even lunchtime,' she moans. 'I hope they won't be wanting food. We've far too much to do, already. It's about time you came back, Ronda. You've been gone for ages. I've had to prepare the haggis all by myself.'

'I'll add to the flavouring,' I say. I will not let Mrs Long tell me how long I can be gone from the kitchen. 'Perhaps you'd like to start on the raspberry cranachan?' I add.

Julie smiles. 'What about me?'

'You're helping me with the rumbledethumps.'

Hugo laughs. 'Are you making up these names?'

'Not at all,' I say in a mock-serious tone. Rumbledethumps practically originated on the Scottish borders.'

'What's in it?' Hugo asks.

'Potato, cabbage and onion. It's a healthy vegetarian dinner option.'

I smile, pleased that I've seen the papers in Herr Schiltz's bedroom, and I've not been caught, and I managed to get out of a sticky situation with Hugo.

I say, 'Now, you'd better go outside into the garden and sort out the fighting warriors. They'll be working up an appetite.'

* * *

When everyone is busy, I slip out of the kitchen. Inside the pantry, I check on the cake. It appears untouched but I look at the fondant carefully for any signs of tampering – I can't take any chances but that's when I hear a muffled scream.

I pause. It's coming from the basement – the dungeon. Instinctively, without thinking, I take the stone steps carefully down where the air is colder and there are soft thumping sounds. My throat dries and I'm reminded of my military experience.

Confidence for life.

The stairs lead me to a tiny passageway at the end of which is an iron door. It isn't closed and I peer through the gap. It's a windowless room that looks as if it's used as a dumping ground for the castle's unused items; old chairs, painting pots and pans. A mixture of dumped rubbish some might call treasure. A bulb swings from the ceiling.

I pause, watching the scene. Gunter and Wilhelm are leaning over Jack, who is lying on the floor.

'Get that rope,' Gunter says. 'We'll tie him up and leave him here.'

'What will Papa say?'

Jack is curled into a foetal position, Gunter kicks him in the kidneys and he groans. 'He won't find out.'

'We can send Freya to rescue him.' Wilhelm laughs. He's struggling with the rope, trying to loop it through the old iron manacles on the wall. 'This will scare her.'

Gunter reaches down and grabs Jack by the neck, places the noose over his head then pushes him close to the wall. Wilhelm tugs on the rope.

'What's happening?' I push open the door and stand with my fists at my side.

'Get out!' Gunter shouts, moving quickly away from Jack.

'Is he alright?' I ask, nodding at Jack's motionless body.

'It's none of your business. Go away!' Wilhelm growls.

Jack whimpers.

'Little pussy, crying for help.' Gunter kicks Jack in the ribs and he groans.

Wilhelm pulls on the rope to lift Jack up.

'STOP!' I shout. 'Leave him alone.' I move forward defiantly. My hands are shaking, but I'm determined.

Wilhelm looks uncertain then he drops the rope and Jack falls on the cold floor, unmoving, and lifeless.

'I'll call your father,' I say. 'He'll know what to do.'

I turn away, but Wilhelm is quick. He moves with the speed of a panther and he grabs me, knocking me flying against the stone wall. I scream in anger, instinctively, twisting. I duck under his shoulder and bring Wilhelm's dominant right arm up behind his back, bending and crushing his wrist, pushing his head against the wall.

Gunter shouts, 'Leave him alone.'

'He hit me.'

'Let him go!' Gunter orders.

'Only when you stop kicking Jack.'

I twist Wilhelm's wrist, and he squeals.

Gunter considers his stepbrother lying with his eyes closed on the floor then he swaggers toward me, smelling of alcohol.

I twist Wilhelm's arm again. 'Help me, Gunter,' he calls.

'I can take you both on if you like. Your father would be very impressed.'

Gunter squares his shoulders and I get ready for him to jump me, but instead, he turns away and heads for the door, sneering at me as he says, 'Bitch! Come on, Wil.' Gunter calls his brother from the steps. 'Let's go. I need a drink.'

I push Wilhelm after him, up the stairs, and he staggers falling and banging his head on the stone step. He glares at me but follows his older brother silently.

After they're gone, I move quickly to Jack's side.

'Are you alright?'

He opens his eyes. 'Have they gone?'

'Yes.'

Jack struggles to sit up, holding his ribs.

'What was that all about?' I ask.

He doesn't reply.

'Are you badly hurt?' I insist.

'It's nothing to do with you. Stay out of it.' I see him wince with pain as he stands up.

'You might have broken ribs. You'll have to rest.'

'It's none of your business.' He straightens up, and with a slight limp, he walks up the steps without a backward glance.

'Well, thank you, Ronda,' I say aloud. 'Thank you for coming to my aid.'

My sarcasm echoes around the dungeon and I wonder what might have happened had I not intervened. I pick up the rope, coil it up and place it with some other dusty junk on a table.

It's a dark and depressing room and I wonder what ill-fate some people may have come to in this place and I shiver. I take a deep breath and I retie my bandana, thinking how good that felt to protect myself against Wilhelm. I might have lost my confidence in the kitchen, but my self-defence instincts are still intact.

* * *

Half an hour later, Paula appears and asks for some lunchtime snacks to be brought to the library. 'Herr Schiltz would like some homemade shortbread and some salmon sandwiches.'

'Oh, would he?' Mrs Long grumbles, forgetting her son's earlier advice about not biting the hand that feeds you. She moans, 'It's all in the picnic hampers. They'll come back half-eaten. It's such a waste.'

'We have some shortbread I put aside in the pantry, we didn't use it all in the hampers,' I say. 'There's also fresh salmon you can use. We are about to make lunch for us anyway, so it's only one extra.'

'He's paying for the food,' says Dan who listened to Mac's advice this morning. 'He can have what he likes.'

Outside the open kitchen window, Bobby the blackbird is chirping happily on the fence. Jim walks past, his eyes glancing everywhere, and he sees me looking at him through the open window.

Suddenly worried, I go to the pantry and check on the birthday cake. I breathe more easily when I see it. It's still exactly how I left it, with the golf ball on the far side against the wall. Nothing has moved. Nothing has been tampered with, and I rub my head and breathe a sigh of relief. I don't trust any of the family. Am I getting paranoid?

* * *

After a snack in the kitchen with the staff, I go back to my room. I'd love a bath, but there's only a shower, and although the power of the water isn't strong, I stand with the water on my back easing the stress and pain in my neck and shoulders.

It was an early start, and I towel myself dry. Although I'm tired, I practise a few kickboxing moves in the privacy of my room to stretch my aching muscles. Then I lie on the bed and reach for the mobile Joachin gave me.

I type quickly.

I've put the diamond ring inside the cake. Couldn't get a photo. They're eating it tonight. It's safe in the pantry. Ronda.

I send the message wondering if Joachin will answer immediately and if he does, hoping we can have a conversation and I can tell him how I was almost caught.

Inspector Joachin texts straight back.

Well done!

I think hard, hoping to engage more with him.

Gunter, Will and Jack have come back early from the grouse hunting. They're arguing. Jack accused Gunter of trying to kill him. Then Gunter and Wilhelm were beating him up. I had to intervene!!

I add the exclamation marks for effect.

Inspector Joachin texts.

Well done. Ronda.

Joachin is a man of few words, so I type.

I was nearly caught in Herr S bedroom but Hugo – the sommelier – saved me and showed me a secret laundry room. Hugo has worked for Herr S before!!

There's no reply and feeling frustrated, I type.

Paula seems to think an announcement will take place tonight and I saw a note in Herr S's bedroom saying, 'I hereby tender my resignation'.

I wait. I keep staring at my phone. Is there anything else I need to tell him?

I read over all the messages again and focus on the positive.

Great job, Ronda – thank you.

I delete the messages. Why am I so needy? So bloody insecure?

This is James's fault. I wasn't like this before. After I won *Masterchef* and I'd done all the interviews and appeared on TV, I had confidence. I knew who I was and where I was going, but then James arrived. He was like a prince, full of praise and love. He was funny, kind and supportive, and when he needed encouragement in his business, he expected that I'd support him. I didn't want to see him low, depressed or worried and when I'd agreed to help, he'd been so pleased. He talked about going to Paris, getting engaged and even married. I'd been such a fool. I'd fallen for his lies. I'd waited for him like an idiot while he'd stolen everything from me. And now, I had to wait for him to pay me back. When I'd tracked him down, I went to his mother's house and told her what happened. She'd cried. She'd pleaded with me. She was old. She loved him, and I'd grown to love her. She'd been kinder to me than my parents – my bullying father and my mother who'd always turned away and pretended nothing was wrong.

I'd adopted James's mother as my own, and I couldn't let her down. I couldn't go to the police. So, although we both knew what James had done was wrong, we had to wait for him to do the right thing, He'd promised us both he would. Six months later, I'm still waiting for the first payment and I'm still bankrupt. Silly Ronda George. I can hear my father's voice, 'You can't handle money. You're useless, Ronda. You'll never be rich. You have to join the army.'

I look at the blank screen in my hand. Joachin hasn't replied so I toss the phone on the bed and close my eyes, feeling suddenly very, very weary – and very, very sad.

Chapter 9

'It is a great act of cleverness to be able to conceal one's being clever.'
Francois de La Rochefoucauld

A soft tapping on the door wakes me. I leap off the bed.

'I thought you'd overslept,' Julie says. 'Mrs Long's had a break, but she's due back in twenty minutes.'

'Wait for me?' I ask. I throw on a clean white tunic and tie a yellow and brown bandana over my hair.

'That looks lovely on you.'

'Thank you.' We are walking back to the kitchen. 'Has anything happened this afternoon?'

'Mac seems very upset, but he's not saying much.'

'He didn't say anything about the others arriving back early?'

Julie shakes her head. 'No, but he seems quite distraught. Perhaps you could speak to him?'

Inside the kitchen, Mac is eating a sandwich taken from one of the picnic hampers lying open beside him on the table.

I pat him companionably on the shoulder. 'Do you want some shortcake?'

He shakes his head.

'Tea?'

He nods, and he remains silent while I make one for us all.

'Want to come outside, and we can drink it on the bench together?'

He glances at Julie, and she smiles encouragingly. 'That's a good idea. That will give me some space. I need to crack on.'

Reluctantly, Mac gets to his feet. He shuffles out of the door behind me, and we sit companionably on the bench at the stone wall.

'I heard there was a row. Some of the guys came back early. Are you alright?'

'I'm okay. Well, I hope so.'

'What do you mean?'

Mac looks uncomfortable. 'It should never have happened.'

'No one was hurt, were they?' I argue.

'But I'm responsible.'

'Do you want to tell me what happened?'

'That's the thing, Ronda. I don't know. One minute everyone is in the butts and the guns are firing and the next thing Gunter is on the moor, unprotected, and then, well, I don't know. He accused Jack of trying to shoot him.'

'Did he?'

'How would you know? How would anyone know what they were doing? I haven't got eyes in the back of my bloody head.'

'Then that's what you should tell Mr Schiltz,' I say with finality.

* * *

The ladies return from their day trip to Loch Ness in a flurry of noise, laughter and general excitement.

Julie helps Mrs Long with the layout for afternoon tea while I go into the pantry, paranoid now about the birthday cake. It hasn't moved. No one has touched it. The golf ball remains in the same place.

'Ronda!'

I jump.

Hugo is standing at the door. 'Want to see something, Ronda?' he whispers.

'Like what?'

'Wow! Is that the birthday cake?' He looks over my shoulder and ventures further into the pantry. 'Did you make that?'

'You know I did. Stop messing with me.'

Hugo grins. 'You mean, you're not falling for my French charm?'

'No.'

'Umm, well how about, I show you something?'

'Thanks for the offer but I haven't time.'

He grins. 'You wish! Come on, it'll take ten minutes, tops – and it's fun! You'll enjoy it.'

'What is it?'

'Come on. Trust me. Where's your sense of adventure?'

'Okay, ten minutes. Lay on, Macduff,' I say.

'And damned be he who first cries, hold enough!'

'Okay, Shakespeare – I'm impressed!'

'You can be my Lady Macbeth.'

'No thanks, she wasn't a very nice person, and things didn't end well for her either.'

I follow him out of the pantry, and he leads me up the back staircase toward the library, but then at the top of the stairs and without any warning, he presses a small hidden lever hidden in the wooden wall panel. There's a slight clunk as secret door swings open.

'Surprise!' he sings quietly. 'Shush, come on.'

'Are you making a habit of this?'

He holds out his hand. 'Come into my parlour, my wee lassie …'

'I'm not a bloody dog,' I reply, wondering if I should even trust him.

* * *

'What if we get caught snooping around?' I whisper.

'We won't. Trust me. They're upstairs in their bedrooms getting changed. They haven't come down to the library yet.'

I step into the dark, narrow passageway behind him, and he hands me his mobile to control the beam of the torch. He pulls the door behind us, and we're trapped like in an Egyptian tomb. I feel claustrophobic. There's no air, and it's hot. My palms begin to sweat. Hugo's mouth is close to my ear.

'We must be very quiet, or they might hear us scurrying around.' He moves cautiously and he guides me carefully along a short pathway. I imagine cobwebs and spiders climbing over my face, and I shudder. He stops suddenly and turns off the torch. He leans closer, toward my ear, and my skin tingles.

'We can see into the library from here, but just in case anyone is in there, I'll turn off the light now. Are you alright?'

'Yes.'

There's a small shaft of light coming into our passageway. Hugo pushes my head toward the spy hole. 'Look!'

I peer through the slatted gap and into the empty library, remembering last night when I was invited into the library to meet the family. Now, Julie and Mrs Long have laid out cakes and teacups, and they have returned to the kitchen.

'What are we hiding behind?' I whisper.

'Books. Do you remember there are rows of books on shelves? Some of them are real, and others are false. Unless you look really closely, you wouldn't know the difference.' He clicks open the secret door into the library. 'Come on. I'll show you.'

Just as he steps into the library, the door opens.

'Quick!' He pushes me back inside. I almost slip, but he holds me by the waist while he secures the secret door, and I feel his rapid breath on my cheek.

It's Louisa's voice we hear first and my body tenses.

'We can talk in here, Fran.'

'I'm sorry, Lou, but this is urgent, and we haven't had a chance to be alone.'

'I know it is difficult. Come on, sit over here near the window. Do you want a drink, Fran?'

'Pour us both one, I think you'll need it,' Fran says seriously.

Their voices are clear and, like Hugo, I lean forward to peer through the slat of light.

Louisa is still wearing navy cut-offs and the pink shirt she had on this morning. She stands at the bar and pours two large Bombay Sapphire gins. She adds a slice of lime, plenty of ice and the small cans of tonic fizz as she pops the top.

'God, I need this,' Fran says. 'Cheers.'

'You're right, Fran. That was a bloody awful day.'

'Whatever is Wilhelm thinking – marrying that bloody American girl. She's a pain.'

'Chloe's not that bad. In fact, I think she might be good for him.'

Fran turns from the window.

'But she'll never be as kind as Roma – how did Gunter manage to marry such a lovely girl? I don't know what she sees in him. She looks positively miserable most of the time. I wish that there was something we could do.'

'It's their marriage so we must leave them to get on with it.'

'She has other options. She could leave him and take the children.'

'He'd make her life miserable. She'd pay a heavy price.' Louisa sips her gin.

'He's so like his father.' Fran moves to the sofa.

Louisa doesn't correct her.

Fran asks, 'What's wrong with Freya, she's always on her phone?'

'I have no idea. I guess it involves someone she's fallen in love with again – but you know what she's like, she's a secretive little devil.'

'Let's sit here, Lou.'

Fran points to a small and uncomfortable sofa where they sit close together, their knees almost touching, and I have to strain to hear their words.

Hugo's rapid, soft breathing near my ear doesn't help, so I dig him in the ribs and put my finger to my mouth, conscious that his taller frame is more cramped in this small space than mine.

Fran says, 'I know that over the years, we've never discussed Mike and Friedrich's business and we both know that they haven't always seen eye to eye on things, but I'm…worried, Lou.'

'What about?'

'Well, I don't know how much Friedrich tells you—'

'I never ask him anything.'

'Well, I don't ask Mike, either, but he left some papers out at home last week. They were on his desk and I—'

'We're you snooping, Fran?' Louisa giggles.

'No, no, I just went into his study, and he'd gone to the bathroom, and I put a cup of coffee on his desk, and I was shocked.'

'Shocked?' Louisa sips her gin. 'Why?'

'Well, you know they've started to export lots of things from the Far East, especially from China?'

'Erm, sort of …'

'Well, do you know or don't you?'

'Friedrich did mention something about it, but I didn't take much notice. Why?'

'Well, you know they normally deal with museums and art galleries, shipping paintings and things like that, well—'

'Get on with it, Fran.' Louisa drains her gin and stands up. 'I haven't got hours, Friedrich expected me upstairs twenty minutes ago. You know what he gets like.'

Fran stands up too. 'Wait! Lou, look, the thing is, I think they're importing animals—'

'Animals?' Louisa looks surprised. 'Have you gone nuts?'

'No, I'm not nuts. And I think it's illegal. I think they're transporting animals that are used illegally, in tests, you know, for pharmaceuticals or makeup and things—'

'Importing into England?'

'No, into the States – into America.'

'You can't be right, Fran. Friedrich would never agree to that. Call him what you like, but he's not a criminal.'

'Then why would Mike have all that paperwork for turtles, reptiles and snakes?'

'Oh, I don't know.' Louisa replaces her glass on the table.

'It's nothing to do with us. We mustn't interfere. Let's go and get changed. We're all meeting at six.' She checks her watch. 'We have less than an hour.'

'But that's not all.' Fran stands her ground, clutching her gin glass. 'The boys were fighting this morning on the moors. Wilhelm is worried that he's being ignored in favour of Gunter—'

'That's nothing new.'

'Yes, but your Jack is furious. Presumably, Friedrich is making a big announcement tonight. Jack thinks that he and Freya are being cut out of any inheritance that Friedrich might leave them.'

'Jack and Freya are *my* children. They have no claim on Friedrich's estate, and they know that.'

'Be honest, Lou, Friedrich has treated your children more favourably than his own boys, and everyone knows it.'

Louisa sighs. 'There's nothing I can do about that.'

'No, you messed up years ago by getting involved with Friedrich in the first place.'

'Don't say that. Not now. Not tonight.'

'Why? It's true. Poor Iris.'

'Don't you DARE!' Louisa shouts.

I pull away from the screen.

She hisses, 'Don't you DARE mention her name. This is *my* birthday party weekend, and I won't be reminded of that woman.'

'I'm sorry, Lou, but you have to open your eyes to see what's going on. Did you know that Friedrich's changing his will?'

'He's not changing his bloody will,' Louisa roars. 'He's NOT.' Then more quietly, she adds, 'He's explaining everything to everyone tonight. Before dinner.'

'But why tonight?'

'Quite simply, my dear Fran, because he wants the truth to come out. The family will have time to assimilate Friedrich's new plans, none of them will create a fuss as it's my birthday, and then tomorrow we will all go home. It will be the end of the matter.'

'I only hope you're right.'

'I am right.'

'We'll see.'

'Come on, Fran. Let's go upstairs and get dressed for dinner. I don't know about you, but I need a shower.'

After they leave the library and I exhale slowly. It's hot in the cramped space, and my tunic is sticking to my back.

'Come on.' Hugo takes my hand and, using the torch, leads me along the narrow pathway back to the back end staircase. He looks out, peering around the secret panel to check the coast is clear, and only after I'm in the passageway does he close the secret door.

Mrs Long appears in that very moment. 'Ronda?'

Suddenly, I'm pushed back against the wall and Hugo is leaning over me smiling. To anyone who didn't know, it might look as if we are kissing.

Hugo says under his breath loud enough for her to hear, 'Oops, Ronda. It looks like our secret is out.'

I glare at him, but he pecks me on the lips and disappears quickly in the opposite direction, leaving the imprint of his quick kiss firmly on my lips.

I bring my hand to my mouth. I haven't been kissed since James.

'Ronda?'

'Yes, Mrs Long.'

'I don't think you have time for this sort of behaviour. The guests are waiting.'

* * *

I say to Dan, 'Would you come and give me a hand?'

He follows me into the pantry.

'Are you going to put it on display while they eat dinner?'

'Yes. Can you make sure no one gets in my way as I carry it through, please?'

I inspect the cake and check the fondant golf ball. The cake is still intact.

'It looks amazing.' Dan then adds with a grin. 'Don't drop it!'

I lift Louisa's birthday cake and carry it carefully, not thinking of the wrath that would descend on me if I dropped it. I can imagine Herr Schiltz's anger. I'd seen my father angry – with my mother – when I was thirteen years old. She had dropped something small, a dish or a plate or something. He'd been furious and he had split her eye open with his fist. I went to help her and she said to me, 'he doesn't mean it, he's a brigadier,' as if a man in his esteemed position wouldn't hit a woman.

A few months later, I'd been carrying a large bag of garden waste to the car. We were going to the dump. The bag split and the anger that my father heaped on me in public had been so humiliating. I can still feel the sting on the back of my legs.

It was something I'd never forgotten.

Dan guides me through to the Grand Hall, to the long table against the near wall, away from the heat and the sunshine. I place the cake on the display stand then rearrange the linen cloth.

'That's amazing, Ronda. I wish you could make me a birthday cake,' Dan says.

'When's your birthday.'

'November.'

'That's a long way off, but if you email me, I'll send you one.'

'Really?'

'Why not?'

'Because … well, no one has ever made me a cake before. Mum bought me one a few times from the supermarket but – it's nothing like this.'

'I'm guessing you'd like one with footballers on it – Celtic?'

Dan laughs and looks pleased. 'You've got to know me, Ronda. You're a good listener.'

If only he knew.

* * *

'Where are the guests now?' Julie asks.

'Arguing as usual.' Hugo appears fed up, so I smile at him.

'Really, what about?' I wipe my hands and look at him.

'They're still in the library, having tea,' he whispers. 'Presumably, Herr Schiltz has some announcement he wants to make, and he wanted to get it over with before the evening started and before Mrs Schiltz's actual birthday celebration tonight.'

'What's he announcing?'

Mrs Long walks into the kitchen and appears flustered. She stops and stares at me chatting to Hugo, and he walks away.

Mac comes in through the back door.

I ask him, 'Have the men patched up the quarrel they had at

106

the grouse shoot?'

Mac frowns. 'They're not men. They're boys.'

'Did they really try to kill each other?' Julie asks.

Mac shrugs. 'Who knows, but they might after the announcement tonight.'

'Why?' Julie asks.

'Presumably, Friedrich Schiltz is stepping down from the company, but he wants Gunter to take over with Jack under his wing.'

'Jack is his stepson?' asks Julie.

'Yes.'

'What about Wilhelm?' I ask.

'That's the problem.' Mac rubs his cheek. 'I think that Wilhelm is working in America. Herr Schiltz wants to close down some of the operations they have over there, you know, minimise the business. He wants more control in Europe so he's favouring his eldest son and stepson who live here.'

'Wilhelm could move back to Europe?'

'He won't. I think he hates his family – and more than anything – he hates his stepmother.'

* * *

I make my escape, and head back to my room, and I dig out Joachin's mobile from my weekend bag.

My text reads.

It's all kicking off. Mr Schiltz is resigning tonight. He wants the business located in Europe. He's putting Gunter and stepson Jack in charge.

I pause, wondering how to say the next part, then I type.

*Wilhelm is p****d off and fighting with Jack – jealous? Fran*

(Mike's wife) told Louisa this pm that Mike is involved in transporting illegal reptiles from China to America – maybe that's a reason?

I press send and wait.

Nothing happens.

I sit thinking about the Schiltz family. My parents had never been kind. After Mum died and I went into the army, my brother had a few more years at boarding school, and instead of joining the military, he took a few menial jobs. He stood up to my father by not contacting him. At the first opportunity, he emigrated to Australia. Although we're not terribly close, I do miss him. And, ironically, since he's been gone we have become even closer with regular online chats.

I stand up and stretch then practise a few kickboxing moves to limber up my aching muscles. When I check again, Joachin still hasn't answered. It's Saturday evening, perhaps he's gone out for dinner with his wife?

I delete my message and hide the phone in my bag before heading back to the kitchen.

Mrs Long looks up when I walk in and by coincidence, one minute later, Hugo walks in behind me. His timing couldn't have been worse but then I think, judging by the mischievous twinkle in his eye, he did it deliberately. Was he following me?

* * *

'Dan,' calls Mrs Long, as I return to the kitchen. 'Can you clear the library, then sort out the table in the Grand Hall? The waiting staff won't be here for another hour.'

Jim the chauffeur strolls into the kitchen. I turn away determined to avoid his gaze. He pulls out a chair at the far end of the table, slips off his jacket and rolls up the sleeves of his shirt. His arms are thick with black hairs and solid muscle, like ham joints.

Mrs Long says, 'Do you want something to eat?'

'Yes.'

'A please wouldn't go amiss,' she mumbles, but Jim ignores her and concentrates on his mobile, waiting for her to serve him. She warms lasagne and adds salad to his plate, and he eats greedily, putting one spoonful after the other into his mouth, his eyes never leaving the mobile screen as he scrolls with his thick finger.

As I walk over to the pantry, I take the opportunity to look over his shoulder. It seems as if he's set up a secret camera. It's a small and grainy picture, but there's a figure moving around. He's monitoring a room. Which one?

'Ronda?'

I turn quickly, and Jim looks up.

Paula hovers in the doorway and beckons for me to join her.

'Are you alright?' I ask.

'Herr Schiltz wants to see you.'

'Me?'

'Yes, now. In the library. He doesn't look very happy.'

My heart begins its familiar unhappy thumping.

Chapter 10

'Seldom ever was any knowledge given to keep, but to impart; the grace of this rich jewel is lost in concealment.'
Wendell Phillips

The library is empty apart from the lone figure of Herr Schiltz. He wanders from the window to the unlit mantelpiece. A massive arrangement of summer flowers, stocks, yellow tulips, red and pink roses, fills the hearth.

'Hello.'

'Sit down, Ronda.'

I close the door and aim for the small sofa where Louisa and Fran sat chatting this afternoon. I take the opportunity to gaze at the bookcase, looking for the spy hole where Hugo and I had listened earlier to their conversation, but I can't see anything.

'Ronda.'

His voice distracts me. 'Yes.'

'I said, sit down there.'

I perch on the edge of the seat, my back straight.

'Were you in my bedroom today?'

'Me?'

'Yes.'

'No.'

'Are you sure?'

'Why?'

Herr Schiltz paces up and down, and I remember my father, the morning I had mustered the courage to tell him I wasn't going to join the army. I had my sights on a cookery course. I had the hotel and catering college prospectus, and there was a year in France where I could practise my skills. I had been beside myself with excitement. I was determined. I had to be true to myself. But my father barely listened. He had other plans for me, and he wasn't about to let me lead my own life, let alone go to France. His voice had been icy, his posture threatening. That's when he'd spat that I was ungrateful, and a liar, and a useless girl with no talent for anything.

'Because someone said they saw you.' Herr Schiltz stops pacing in front of me, and I'm forced to look up at him.

'Who?' My heart is hammering.

'It doesn't matter.'

'How could they?' I have to challenge him. I have to stand my ground. But I'm thinking of Jim and the video images that he was studying in the kitchen. 'Well, I wasn't there.'

'You were on the battlements this morning with Hugo.'

I stare at him. 'Yes.'

'How did you get up there?'

I stand up.

'I'm a chef, Herr Schiltz. You asked me here to cater for you and your family. I'm not here to be interrogated about my whereabouts every minute of the weekend, but I'll be honest. I have spent time with Hugo, and he insisted on showing me the spectacular view from there.'

'How did you get up there?'

I stare at him.

I don't want to involve Hugo until I've had a chance to speak to him and we both tell the same story.

'I think you should ask your chauffeur these questions. He seems to know everything.' Herr Schiltz looks taken aback. 'He's the one who is in the kitchen watching people on remote cameras that he's planted around the castle—'

'That's none of your business. Jim's done it now, under my instruction because of the invasion of my privacy.'

'Then if that's how you want to behave – spying on your family – then go ahead. But please don't involve me in your petty family scandals because I have nothing to gain or lose. I'm not interested.'

He looks affronted, and he blinks.

I continue, 'Now, I'm going back to the kitchen to finish off the birthday meal for your wife. And, I'd appreciate your discretion with my friendship with Hugo because Mrs Long is looking for a reason to be angry with me, other than the fact that I've taken over her kitchen. You might have your family scandals and politics, but like in Downtown Abbey, this is no different. The staff downstairs also have their political agendas …'

I'm warming up now and I'm in full flow.

'To be honest, Herr Schiltz, all I want is to be professional.'

I face him, dressed in my whites, with my bandana still tied around my spiked hair. My face, I know, is filled with anger, pride and determination just as it should have been when I faced my father over ten years ago.

'Right, go back to the kitchen,' he says, obviously determined to stay in control.

I'm on a roll, and I want to cement my newfound confidence

when I see a movement. It's a very slight shift, over his right shoulder, in the bookcase. I know that we're being watched, not by a camera hidden in the room by Jim, but by someone hiding in the secret passageway behind the bookshelf.

I could call out. I could name and shame, but I don't. I walk out of the room, wondering if Hugo had witnessed our complete exchange.

* * *

Mac wanders aimlessly around the kitchen but manages to stay out of our way. 'I believe Herr Schiltz was holding individual meetings with everyone. I think he's told them his future plans.'

'That's good, isn't it?' Julie glances up.

Mac shakes his head morosely. 'I have a feeling that thunder is on the way.'

I monitor and check each course.

Julie helps me, working under my direction, and we work well as a team.

As I enter the Grand Hall with the first course, Hugo follows me to explain the choice of wines with each meal. I smile, and he winks back.

I make a point of serving Herr and Frau Schiltz first, and while he studiously ignores me.

Louisa beams delightedly.

'My goodness, thank you, Ronda. This looks delightful,' she exclaims, and she leads a smattering of applause. 'So, this is the grouse the men shot today?'

'Yes,' I reply.

'Did you cook it whole?' asks Fran.

'I removed the wishbone and legs as they cook quicker otherwise they might dry out.'

'What's the sauce?' Gunter asks.

There isn't a hint of our earlier encounter in the small hall.

'The brambles are garnishing. I fried off the grouse in butter and thyme and popped it in the oven for a few minutes. Then I sautéed the mushrooms, spinach and watercress. There's some blackberry jam if you like or gravy if you prefer.'

There's a spontaneous burst of applause led by Roma.

I smile gratefully.

By the time I return with dessert, Scottish raspberry cranachan, the guests' voices have risen several decibels. Fine champagne and wine have been consumed, and their voices seem louder, more querulous.

Herr Schiltz taps a knife on the crystal glass and asks for silence.

'I'm sure you will all agree with me when I say this is probably one of the best meals we've ever enjoyed in Scotland, so please give Ronda a round of applause.'

I pause at the doorway. I suspect it's the only meal, apart from last night, they've eaten in Scotland.

The guests clap, and even Jack and Wilhelm who sit at opposite ends of the table applaud cheerfully. They all seem a little drunk apart from Freya who has her mobile at her fingertips.

'Thank you. It's been my pleasure.' I make a small bow. 'But we're a team in the kitchen. I couldn't have done it without them.'

'I love your bandanas,' Fran shouts, applauding.

I smile and, as the clapping dies down, I make my escape back to the kitchen.

Mac is leaning against the sink, near the back door with his arms folded.

'You're popular,' he says.

'They love Scottish food,' I whisper, smiling.

'What's your secret then?'

'Fine quality honey and a single malt whisky.'

He nods. 'I'm impressed.'

'Mrs Long should be out there with me, but there wasn't time to call you all in.'

Mrs Long straightens her back. 'There's never any thanks in this business.' She takes off her apron and tosses it on the back of the chair vacated earlier by Jim and says, 'I'm calling it a night. I haven't been out of the kitchen all day, not like some people.' She glares at me, and I wonder if she wants me to challenge her, so I smile.

'Have a lovely evening, Mrs Long.' I wonder if she's hurrying home to her husband, Mac's father.

'There's not much left of it.' She picks up her handbag, and as she passes Mac, she mutters, 'I'm going to call in on Maggie. I want to make sure she's alright.'

'Maggie?' I ask him.

He raises his eyes to the ceiling. 'My ex. They get on.'

I grin back at him.

'Where's Jim?' I ask.

'He's back upstairs, prowling as he does.' Mac glances out of the window, distracted.

'Prowling?'

'I caught him last night out near the stables after you'd gone to bed. He said he was stretching his legs, but I swear that guy has got eyes in the back of his head. I swear it. He must be military trained. He hears everything.'

'Really?' My mouth goes dry.

'He reckoned someone was upstairs in Mr Schiltz's bedroom this morning.'

'Weren't all the guests out?'

'That's what I said. I said it was probably Cheryl and her sister, they do the cleaning, but he wasn't having any of it.'

'Oh.' I'm not sure what to say.

'He said he saw you and Hugo on the battlements.'

I turn and smile. 'Yes, I wanted to see the view.'

'I think he likes you.'

'Who? Jim?'

Mac smirks. 'You know perfectly well I mean Hugo, Ronda George!'

* * *

While they finish dinner, I head outside, where the setting sun is casting a beautiful pink and mauve glow over the sky and the trees beyond.

I sit on the bench beside the garden wall and check my watch. Nine-thirty.

Julie comes outside. 'Can I sit with you?'

'Of course.'

She pulls a packet of cigarettes from her pocket. 'I shouldn't, I know but, oh well...' She flicks the lighter and inhales deeply.

'Do you enjoy working here?'

'Most of the time. This weekend has been one of the best. I've had a break from the place where I rent. It's nice out here. It's the proper countryside.'

'It is lovely.'

'Do you like Mac?' she asks.

I look at her flushed face.

'He seems a very nice man.'

She flicks an imaginary piece of ash from her skirt. 'He's asked me out.'

'Good.'

'He's at least five years younger than me.'

'So?'

'What would Mrs Long say?'

I shrug. 'It's none of her business but to be honest with you, she should be very honoured and proud that her son has found a lovely woman to take out on a date.'

Julie giggles. 'It's not a date, but I'm not sure.'

'Are you married?'

'Divorced. Hamish and I barely lasted two years.'

'Well, Mac's single now too.'

Julie nods, stubs out her cigarette and hides the butt behind a dead leaf in the earth. She stands up.

'I'll come inside in a minute,' I say.

Just as she leaves, Hugo appears.

'I was looking for you,' he says.

'Why?'

He slides onto the bench and sits close beside me. 'What did you think of that conversation this afternoon?'

'I don't know. I guess it's none of my business.'

'They're a strange family, aren't they?'

I lean my head back against the brickwork and close my eyes.

'Tired?' he asks.

'A little.'

'Do you want to come upstairs to the battlements and see the sunset?'

'We can't do that. We are not guests.' I grin at his eagerness. 'How about after they've eaten the birthday cake? You organise a bottle of Chablis for the workers, and I'll organise us some food?'

'You're only after me for the wine.'

'True – I suppose a bottle of champagne is out of the question.' I smile.

'Off-limits.' He nods thoughtfully.

'Did Herr Schiltz make his grand announcement?' I ask.

'Yes.'

'Well, it's quiet. No fights. They seem to have taken the news well.'

'On the surface, yes.'

'What do you mean?'

'Some of them have been doing shots. They're heavy drinkers.'

Dan puts his head out of the kitchen door and calls out.

'I don't want anything to eat. Is it alright if I go? Can I leave early?' He grins. 'Before it all hits the fan.'

* * *

When I return to the kitchen, Mrs Long is in a panic.

'Ronda? Where were you? They've been looking for you. They want you in the Grand Hall immediately.'

I stare at her. 'Me?'

'The cake, they want to cut it now and they want you there. Hurry up! Now!'

I put my hands to my bandana and straighten it up.

'Leave that, you look fine. It's bad enough that Hugo had disappeared but you as well, hurry up.'

Paula escorts me to the dining hall where Hugo is busy serving glasses of chilled Dom Pérignon.

'Ah, Ronda,' Herr Schiltz says, 'Come over here and stand with us. This is a great photo opportunity for you all.'

Freya, Roma and Jack take the hint and lift their phone cameras and stand up from the table.

I shuffle up beside him, trying to smile.

'I won't eat you,' Herr Schiltz adds, his excellent humour obviously restored.

I smile, but it's as fake as the castle paintings above our heads.

'Gather around.' He beckons to everyone, and suddenly chairs are scraped back, and we're surrounded by family.

'Fab cake, Ronda.' Freya smiles at me and, encouraged, I smile back. She clicks a photo.

'You've done an amazing job, Ronda. Look! There's even a golf buggy, how clever of you. I love it.' Louisa claps her hands together.

I smile.

They exclaim their delight and heap praise on the cake, but my mouth is as dry as a summer's day.

Herr Schiltz picks up the cake knife, and he turns to me.

'There are no surprises, are there, Ronda?'

I can't speak. My fake smile freezes, and suddenly I have this awful feeling that I've been played. I've been cheated.

Herr Schiltz knows that I'm the only one who's aware of the ring hidden in the cake, but he seems to be laughing at me.

The family gather around.

Jim takes a step closer.

'Come on, my dear Louisa. My birthday girl. Let's cut your cake together.'

There's a smattering of *oohs* and *ahhhs* and applause as Herr

Schiltz takes his wife's hand as if it's their wedding day, and he places it with his hand on the hilt of the knife.

It doesn't look right.

I hold my breath.

They cut a wedge with the fondant golf ball on top and he slides it onto a plate.

Herr Schiltz frowns. He tilts his head, examining the sponge and, from his expression, I know there's something wrong.

The ring is gone.

Chapter 11

'Talking much about oneself can also be a means to conceal oneself.'

Friedrich Nietzsche

'This looks delightful,' Louisa exclaims. 'My favourite – sponge cake. How lovely.' Louisa holds the plate and takes a small bite. 'Absolutely delicious!' she cries.

Herr Schiltz glares at me. His face is thunderous. He waves the knife, and Jim steps closer, knowing something is wrong.

I swallow hard. My face is flushed. One by one, the guests realise Herr Schiltz isn't happy, and they turn to follow his gaze.

They're all staring at me.

Louisa looks at her husband and then at me as she senses something's wrong too.

'Darling?' she says. 'Friedrich?'

'There's supposed to be a surprise for you—'

I shake my head. How can I explain? It's impossible. I've checked. There was no way anyone could have taken off the fondant and replaced it with such accuracy.

I step forward to look at the sponge. How could anyone have tampered with it?

'Perhaps I could cut the next slice.'

I take the knife from his hand and cut into the cake.

'I don't think you had the right slice.'

I cut firmly and slice another wedge of sponge and place it on another plate.

Herr Schiltz begins examining it. There's a flash, a bright blue diamond.

To my relief, his faces breaks into a smile.

'Ronda is right, my dear Louisa. I didn't quite cut the right piece for you.'

'Whatever do you mean, darling?'

Louisa reluctantly lets go of the first plate and takes the second one, looking at it quizzically and then her face breaks out into a broad and happy smile.

'Oh, my goodness. Friedrich, what's this?'

'What is it?' asks Freya.

'Is it a surprise?' Fran asks.

'It's probably something expensive,' adds Wilhelm.

'Oh, goodness. I don't believe it.' Louisa pulls the valuable ring from the sponge, places it in her mouth and sucks the mixture from the precious stones as if she's done it all before, and then pulls it from her mouth. 'There, that's lovely and clean now.'

She places it onto the third finger on her right hand and holds it up. 'It's magnificent, Friedrich. What a lovely surprise.'

'Let me have a look,' says Roma, pushing forward.

'That's a proper rock.' Chloe nudges Wilhelm. 'That's what you call a *real* diamond,' she drawls, and he snorts irritably.

Herr Schiltz beams as Louisa kisses him on the cheek.

'You really do know how to treat your wife,' Fran says. 'Well done, Friedrich!'

'That's a lovely gesture,' agrees Mike.

Only Gunter and Jack remain silent.

Meanwhile, Jim hovers menacingly over my shoulder, and I feel that I have a reprieve from the death sentence.

* * *

I'm alone in the kitchen.

Mrs Long has gone home. Dan and the waiting staff have left for the evening.

Julie agrees to do a circuit of the rooms and corridors looking for dirty glasses while I search the fridge to find some supper for Julie, Hugo and possibly Paula when there's a noise behind me.

I look up, expecting Hugo, and I'm shocked to see Gunter.

He says, 'My father doesn't trust you.'

I close the fridge door and straighten my shoulders. He has milky blue eyes, red-rimmed and bloodshot. Hugo said earlier some of the family had been downing shots, and I guess Gunter is one of them.

'I don't care about your father. I'm here to cook, nothing more and nothing less. Is there something you want here?'

'What would you have to gain?' He leans against the worktop, folds his arms but seems to find it hard to maintain his balance, and regards me thoughtfully. 'Why would you want to read the documents in my father's bedroom?'

'If there's nothing else you want, then I suggest you leave, go back upstairs and join your family.'

He sighs heavily. 'Do you know what it's like working for a man like my father?'

'Yes.'

He looks surprised.

'My father was exactly the same,' I add.

'Really?' His laugh is patronising and he sneers. 'You had a multi-billion pound business to run, did you?'

'That's not the point. The point is, their characters are the same.'

'What's my father's character?'

'The same as yours.'

Gunter laughs and steps closer to me. 'You're a cheeky little bitch.' He grabs my wrists.

'I wouldn't do that if I were you,' I warn him.

He laughs and lets me go.

'I didn't ask you to come into my kitchen, and I'd like you to go now.'

'I'll do what I like. Get me a coffee.'

'There are staff upstairs who will get you coffee.' I'm thinking of Hugo and Julie, who I will enlist for support.

'You don't like taking orders, do you?'

'That's not the point. If you go upstairs, I'll get someone to bring your coffee up to you.'

Hugo walks in and stops in surprise when he sees the stand-off between us.

'Mr Schiltz, can I get you something?'

'Mr Schiltz would like coffee,' I say.

'I'll bring it upstairs to you. Let's leave the ladies to sort the kitchen out,' Hugo says smoothly, 'Would you like a liqueur or brandy with that?'

I raise my eyebrows. He's clearly had enough to drink, but I guess this is Hugo's way of enticing him away.

'Jim is keeping an eye on everything,' Gunter says. 'He knows where you all are, and what you are all doing, so be careful –

I'm warning you all.'

'Thank you,' Hugo says. 'It's good to know we're all being taken care of.' Hugo moves to stand between us, effectively blocking Gunter from coming closer to me.

Gunter seems to get the message that Hugo isn't moving and when he's out of earshot I say, 'Drunken idiot.'

Hugo looks at me. 'What was all that about?' he asks.

I shrug.

Hugo is watching me. His gaze doesn't leave my face.

'Jim thinks I was in Herr Schiltz's bedroom. They saw us together on the battlements.'

I give all this information to Hugo, hoping that he will take my cue and understand the subtle message I'm giving him.

'That's none of their business,' Hugo says curtly.

'That's what I told Herr Schiltz,' I reply, but I can't stop the unease growing in my stomach.

Julie comes in the back door smelling faintly of cigarettes. I frown. Why was she outside smoking when I thought she was upstairs collecting the dirty glasses?

* * *

Hugo is called onto the terrace of the Grand Hall where Louisa, Herr Schiltz, Fran and Mike are seated around a terrace table. They have also asked for coffee which Julie takes to them. I'm now feeling courageous, so I carry Gunter's coffee upstairs to the library.

I push open the door, but the room is empty. I'm about to leave when I hear the soft sounds of whimpering. I pause.

Is it an animal?

'Hello?' I whisper.

No one replies. Fleetingly, I wonder if the room is haunted, but then a small voice asks, 'Have you ever been in love?'

I close the library door behind me and walk over to a silhouette on the couch, furthest from the window, where a young girl is curled in a foetal position. Her hair is a mess, and mascara has smeared her cheeks.

'Yes. I have.'

'Isn't it awful?'

'Yes. Terrible.' I place the coffee on the table.

'Is that for me?'

'You can have it if you like, I can always make another one.'

'Who is it for?'

'Gunter?'

'Oh, him. Well, in that case, I'll drink it. Sod him.'

I grin. 'Don't you get on with Gunter?'

'He doesn't like Jack or me. He reckons I'm spoilt and Jack's lazy.'

'Is that true?'

Freya swings her legs off the sofa and reaches for the cup. 'I was doing shots with Wil – Wilhelm – and now I feel terrible.'

'Then, why do it?'

'You can't show any weakness, or they bully you.' She sips the coffee gratefully. 'They're awful.'

I turn to leave. I'd better make Gunter more coffee, or he will be even more annoyed.

'Ronda?'

'Yes.'

'Are you in love now?'

'No.'

'It's better that way, isn't it?'

'Much better.'

'They can't hurt you then, can they?'

'No.'

Frey begins to cry again, and instinctively I sit down beside her. She leans against me. I put my arm around her shoulder. 'Do you want to tell me about it?' I'm curious, but I'm not sure if I need an outpouring of grief about love right at this moment. After my experience with James, I'm probably not the best person to advise her either.

'I'd probably shock you.'

'I doubt it.'

'Do you know Paula?'

'Yes.'

'We had a fling last month. We met in London, in a club and one thing led to another, but when she found out that I was her boss's stepdaughter, she got scared and she called it all off.'

I take a deep breath. 'Well, that's awkward.'

'I thought I was over her until yesterday when I saw her again. It's awful even being in the same room as her – and then, even worse, Jack started flirting with her.'

'Doesn't he know she's gay?'

'No one does. She's not out.'

'Are you?'

'Yes, pretty much, but no one talks about it apart from Gunter who said over dinner that I needed a man and a good seeing to—'

'Charming.'

'I know. That's why I don't talk about it.'

'What about your mum, have you spoken to her?'

'Yes, and she told me not to mention it to Friedrich, or anyone. She said some things should remain private. I don't think she knows what to do.'

'It's complicated.'

'None of them really cares, and now with Friedrich's announcement today, it's all hit the fan anyway.'

'What announcement?'

Freya looks at me and then says, 'I guess it's common knowledge now, but he's resigning from the board.'

'Is that a shock?'

'Yes. A massive one. I think Mum is upset.'

'Why?'

Freya frowns. 'I don't know, but it means that he's focusing on the business in Europe, while Mike wants to branch out in America. It's dividing the family. Gunter will take over in Europe, and they will have to move to London and Roma is fed up. She likes living in Berlin. I heard them arguing last night after we arrived.'

I remember how Roma had looked upset and sad.

'I'm sure it will all get sorted out,' I say. 'Everything works out in the end.'

'It won't,' she wails. 'We've only just started to get normal after the last; you know the last …'

'The last what?' I encourage her.

Freya runs her hand through her hair. 'Oh God, don't tell me you don't know! You must be the only one in the bloody castle who doesn't…'

I shrug. 'Sorry … but now I'm curious. Know what?' I probe.

'Friedrich's first wife – Iris – died. She was killed. Shot dead. There were so many rumours at the time, and we really suffered.'

'Who?'

'Me and Jack. You see, Louisa, our mum, and Friedrich were having an affair for almost ten years. We didn't know. Jack and I were young and we were at school. But then when the police started investigating, it all came out. There was talk about a cover-up and police corruption. It was awful. Our lives were picked apart by the media and I hated it all. My mum was called all sorts of things, and then my dad divorced her and she *had* to marry Friedrich then. I think she did it to save our reputation.'

'And did they catch the person who killed Iris?' I ask, remembering the scant details that Inspector Joachin had told me in the pub in London.

'They arrested their gardener. They said Iris was having an affair with him and she wanted to call it off, but he was jealous, so he shot her. But the thing is, he didn't do it.'

'How do you know that?'

'Mum told me soon afterwards. She was distraught. Dad left, and she was alone. She said they were hiding things, and then afterwards she had no choice. Her affair with Friedrich became public, and now she's stuck with him.'

'But she doesn't love him?' I'm thinking of the blue diamond, the present in her birthday cake.

'Could *you* love him?' Freya replies quickly.

I take a deep breath. 'It's not about me.'

'I know, but don't you see, Ronda? We're stuck with him and this awful family.'

'You can go off to university soon and live somewhere else or go abroad.'

'I want to live in London, but I don't know what will happen now that Friedrich is retiring. He'll have even more control over us all ...'

I wish Freya wasn't slurring her words so much.

'He'll force me to go to Germany.'

'Maybe you can—'

'Don't you understand?' Freya's face crinkles in frustration. 'Herr Schiltz knows who did it. He knows who killed his first wife, but he won't say. He's covering up for someone.'

'Who?'

'Who do you think?' Freya pulls away and pulls a tissue from her pocket. She wipes her eyes and dabs at the mascara stain, and as she does that I see a slight movement behind the hidden bookshelf, then there's a scuffle and silent curse.

'Who's there?' I call out.

Freya follows my gaze. We both sit up.

'Come on out!' I say, raising my voice. 'We all know about the secret passage.'

Freya says, 'Perhaps they're stuck.'

In a few strides, I'm at the secret library panel. I push the particular book with the lever, and the door clicks open, and Wilhelm falls into the room laughing. He can barely stand.

'He's drunk,' says Freya. 'Spying on us, were you?'

'Just checking to see what woman you're kissing now.' Wilhelm laughs tauntingly, and it takes me all my trained army discipline not to kick him in the nuts.

* * *

I can't leave the library fast enough. My conversation with Freya was exciting, but I don't want to get involved in Freya and Wilhelm's drunken arguments.

I'm half-way down the stairs when I hear Freya leave the library and slam the door behind her.

In the kitchen, Hugo says,' Where were you?'

'I took coffee up to Gunter, but then I found Freya in the

library whose need was greater than his.'

Hugo nods. 'She was downing lots of shots.'

I make a fresh coffee and return upstairs with the tray, just as Jim enters the kitchen. I don't want to be left alone with him, and I take the stairs two at a time.

Outside on the battlements, the air is chilled. I take a quick look at the magnificent view. The setting sun has left a magenta and crimson sky, the clouds are like an artist's palette. It would be lovely to share the view with someone special.

'Hey, over here.' I turn to see Gunter lying on a sun-bed beside his wife. He points at a table.' Put it there.'

Wordlessly I place the tray on the table, and I turn away.

'It's Ronda, isn't it?' Roma sits up and pulls a shawl around her shoulders. 'That meal you cooked. All the meals have been delicious. Thank you.'

The tip of cigar flares up and in the dusk, I see a vague outline of a shadow.

'You're welcome.' I stand for a second feeling sorry for Roma. She continues to smile at me, as if she wants a conversation, almost as if she's grateful.

'You shouldn't have to do that.' Mike's voice is louder than I expect. 'You shouldn't have to bring that up here. Aren't there any waiters to do that?'

'They've gone off duty.'

Mike sniffs. 'Well, the family can help themselves if they want anything. You've all worked so hard. You must be exhausted.'

'That's true.' I smile.

'Where's Jim?' Gunter asks Mike.

Although he's not asking me, I reply, 'He's just gone into the kitchen.'

'Probably spying on someone else,' Mike says, 'and it will make a change that it isn't Fran or me that he's filming. She's distraught. He frightened her earlier. He prowls around like he's an undercover spy working for MI5, but he's a thug. I don't know why Friedrich trusts him – all this talk of someone in his room – it was probably Jim.'

Gunter says slowly, 'There's something not right. Papa did say he wanted us to relocate to London. Still, it's not normal for Dad to want to resign like this, without mentioning it to any of us before …' He glares at me as if I should have left by now so I walk away, but I pause out of sight near the door to the stairs and wait, listening.

'He's asking us to uproot our life, move to London without even discussing it with us first,' Roma complains.

'He told me on Friday after we arrived.' Gunter's tone is rude.

'Yes, and you told me. But I'm not happy,' Roma replies. 'What about our children and their friends in Germany and their education?'

'Shut up, Roma,' Gunter says. 'I'm sick of going through all of this with you. You knew when you married me what it would be like—'

'I never expected you to be at your father's beck and call. It was bad enough after your mother died and what we all went through, with all the public humiliation, but this is—'

'Roma, stop. That's enough. That's my mother you're talking about.'

'I know.'

'Speak about her with some respect.' Gunter is angry.

'Respect?' Roma scoffs. 'Neither you, nor your brother, or even Friedrich treated her with respect. You were awful to her, you *all* mistreated her. She was too frightened to stand up to you but don't think I'm going to be like that. You're not going to behave like that to me, Gunter – if you don't treat me with respect – if *any* of you don't treat me with respect then I'll be gone, and I'll take my children with me.'

'And where would you go?' Gunter laughs.

'I'll find somewhere – and don't fool yourself. I'll find someone who will love me properly.'

'Like Jim?' Gunter teases.

'Jim?' repeats Mike.

'He's got a crush on Roma – that's his excuse to film us all – so that he can secretly spy on my wife. Rather like you, Mike. You'd have a go at her, wouldn't you?'

'You're disgusting,' Roma says, and I hear her standing up. 'You're drunk.'

A waft of cigar smoke drifts toward me. I swallow a cough before dashing through the doorway and into the darkness of the castle stairwell. I'm dashing down the flights of stone steps when suddenly a hand grabs my wrist, and Wilhelm pulls me violently against my will, into the vast space of the small hall.

Chapter 12

'And when a woman's will is as strong as the man's who wants to govern her, half her strength must be concealment.'
George Eliot

Wilhelm holds both my wrists together. His face is close to mine as he kicks the door closed behind us and pushes me against the wall. His breath is rank; stale alcohol and garlic.

'What were you doing up on the battlements?'

'Nothing.' I pull from his grip.

'You were listening to their conversation? You're spying on us, aren't you? That's why you came down to the dungeon.' He throws me back against the wall, but I slip and fall against the old tapestry. I'm rubbing my wrists when he asks, 'Well? What were you doing up there?'

'I took coffee to your brother.'

'A likely story.'

I stare at him. 'Then go and check. Go and ask them.'

'You also took coffee to Freya, are you the new coffee maid?' He laughs.

'A lot of the staff have gone home. I'm helping.'

He leans forward. His breath rushes at me when he says, 'You were eavesdropping. I saw you. Why?'

I sigh dramatically. 'Look, I'm exhausted. Gunter asked me to take him up a coffee to the battlements. It's a beautiful evening, and I haven't been out of the kitchen for a—'

'You're a liar. You were in the library with Freya.'

'Because,' I say with exaggerated patience. 'I was looking for Gunter.'

He leans closer, and I step back.

'You're a liar.'

'It's always been my experience that when someone accuses you of something – it's because it's their own weakness.'

'You're a bitch.'

'And you spy on people using the secret passageways, only you're not even good at that, we heard you.'

'Are you a lesbian too?' he taunts.

'It's none of your business.' I smile.

'Freya doesn't like men.'

'Freya does like men; she just doesn't want to sleep with them all.'

He laughs loudly. 'She's a dyke.'

I turn to walk away, but he grabs my shoulder and spins me around. 'Don't turn your back on me. I'm talking to you.'

'It's been a long day, and I'm up again early tomorrow.'

'Do you want to have sex?'

I laugh with surprise. 'No, thanks.'

He pulls at his belt. 'I've got something here …'

'Save it for Chloe, I'm sure she can't resist your charms, besides, where is she?' I ask to distract him.

He's unbuttoning his fly, but he's still drunk, and his fingers can't coordinate. He frowns. Then suddenly, he reaches out and grabs my arm. 'Help me.' His grip is tight. He places my hand on his cock.

I twist quickly, turn and elbow him in the ribs, then I take a few steps back and sidekick him in the lower stomach.

He doubles over.

Taking up my kickboxing stance, I double-punch him in the face, spin around and land him a kick on the back of his calf.

He slumps to the floor.

I walk out and close the door behind me, trying to ignore my racing heart.

* * *

Julie is in the kitchen, humming to herself when I walk in. She looks weary.

'You took your time, Ronda. Is everything alright?'

'I got delayed.'

'Are you okay?'

'Yes.'

'Mac said the family are all drunk and angry.'

'I think he's right. Where is he?'

'Trying to keep an eye on them all without upsetting them. He's frightened they might make a mess or ruin something in the castle, and they're all paranoid about being watched.'

'Roll on tomorrow afternoon,' I grin. 'Right, let's have some supper, shall we?'

I spend a few minutes looking in the fridge and the pantry before reappearing with smoked salmon, langoustines, guacamole, various cheeses and fresh rolls. I've just placed the food on the table when Hugo walks in. He grins at the array of food in appreciation.

'You can only eat with us if you provide us with a bottle of something delicious.'

'With alcohol content,' Julie adds.

Hugo returns a few minutes later with a chilled bottle of Chardonnay. 'Am I accepted into the girly kitchen club?'

'I'll have to ask my colleague. Julie, is Hugo allowed to join us?'

She grins at our pantomime. 'Of course, now that he's brought refreshments.'

Hugo stands behind us and pours the wine professionally. 'Would madam like to sample the wine?'

'No!' Julie and I cry out in unison.

'Just pour it out,' she adds, 'quickly.'

'That's been a day,' I say, sipping the wine with appreciation. 'We'll all sleep well tonight.'

'So long as Jim isn't prowling around outside again like he did last night.' Julie takes a langoustine. 'Doesn't that man sleep at all?'

'I think a lot of them will be up all night.' Hugo helps himself to smoked salmon and guacamole. 'Herr Schiltz's resignation seems to have sent them into a panic. Mike is on the terrace trying to get him to change his mind – but he's resolute.'

'An unmitigated disaster,' I say, savouring the wine on my tongue. 'For a birthday weekend.'

'Do you think it's deliberate?' asks Hugo.

'Why would he ruin his wife's birthday?' Julie asks.

I think of the conversation with Freya, and if it's true what she said that Louisa is staying with her husband because she has to, then maybe he knows this. But perhaps deep down, *he* loves her.

'I think he genuinely wants her to have a happy birthday.' I think of the diamond ring hidden in the birthday cake.

'I don't think he's the sort of man to consider anyone,' says

Julie. 'He seems to do what he wants, whenever he wants to, just like his sons.'

'Where's Jack?' I ask.

It's Julie who replies. 'I was out having a cigarette I saw him walking around the grounds with Chloe.'

'Wilhelm got annoyed with Jack, and he started drinking shots, challenging Gunter and Freya …' Hugo's sentence drifts, and his face darkens. I turn around to follow his gaze and look over my shoulder.

Jim's body fills the doorway.

'Have you got any ice?'

Hugo stands up quickly. 'An ice bucket? Of course.'

'Not a bucket, I just want ice.' Jim stares at the feast on the table. 'Someone has beaten the shit out of Wilhelm. It's to take the bruising out of his cheek.'

I don't say a word. I concentrate on the shell of the langoustines, hoping my face won't give me away, wondering if Wilhelm will admit to being hit by a woman.

'What happened?' Julie asks.

'Someone must have got sick of his smart mouth,' Jim replies. 'But they won't get away with it. They're like a clan, this family, if you hurt one, you hurt them all – once they find out who did it, then there will be a price to pay.'

My heart is thumping rapidly. I don't look up.

'It's probably one of the family members,' Hugo replies, passing Jim a bowl of ice and a clean tea towel. 'No one else would have a motive for that kind of behaviour, unless of course…' he pauses. 'Wilhelm provoked someone.'

Jim takes the ice and leaves without replying.

* * *

By the time I make my way back to my room in the converted stables, I'm more than weary. It's been a long day. Inside my room, it feels different. I look around, check the small wardrobe, my overnight bag and the bathroom but all seems untouched. I look around the walls, paranoia taking hold of me, wondering if Jim has planted a camera in my room, but I find nothing.

Satisfied with my investigation, I shower quickly and then lie on my bed, and check my mobile messages. There are three from Tina with a couple of photos of Molly. I smile and spend a while looking at their silly faces. In one image, they both have their tongues hanging out, and I laugh aloud.

I reach for the second phone hidden in my weekend bag, the phone Inspector Joachin gave me, and there's one message waiting for me.

You've done a great job today. Thank you. We are so close to the information we need. There's just one more favour I have to ask you to do. Message me when you can. It doesn't matter what time it is.

I sigh.

One more favour; I want to go home. I want to be in London.

I type slowly, my eyes closing.

Strange family. Angry and mostly drunk. Herr Schiltz has resigned from the board, and this has tipped them over the edge. They all have their issues. Mrs S liked the ring!!

I pause. There's a lot of information to write.

Herr S is closing the USA office. Gunter and Roma have to relocate to London, rumour has it Gunter must work with Jack, but they hate each other. Freya said that Herr S knows who killed his first wife. Jim is spying on everyone. What do you want me to do?

Inspector Joachin replies right away.

There's a package taped under your bed. Please can you put it beside Herr Schiltz's breakfast plate in the morning – without getting caught!

There's a package under my bed.

Who's been in my room?

I'm so tired I almost roll onto the floor, and just as Inspector Joachin described there's a brown padded envelope taped to the springs under my bed. It's the size of an envelope that would hold a hardback book. I decide to leave it there.

I turn off the light, and I'm so tired, I fall asleep immediately.

* * *

I wake early and with a start. Inspector Joachin's phone is still on the duvet beside me, and my own phone is on the small table. I check them both – no new messages.

I read Inspector Joachin's message from last night again, and I remember how I'd been too tired to react to his last favour. I delete the messages.

I pull back the duvet and kneel on the floor. The package is held by thick masking tape to the bed frame springs.

The padded envelope is shaped like a book. I touch it like an excited child would maul a present on Christmas Eve, but I feel suddenly uneasy. It isn't a book.

I shove it under the duvet; then I pull on my shorts, t-shirt and my running shoes. I make an effort with a few stretches then when I open the door, the first glimpse of dawn takes my breath away.

It's beautiful; golden light shines on the tips of the firs along the riverbank, and the birdsong is as loud as an opera. It's simply stunning.

I run for forty minutes, and by the time I return to my room, my body is damp with perspiration. I shower and tie a red, cream and golden bandana around my wet hair. I pull on clean chef whites and shove Inspector Joachin's package into the deep pocket, wondering how I can place this on the dining table without Jim or one of his many cameras noticing me.

* * *

It's five-thirty and Bobby the blackbird is chirping happily on the fence, but all is quiet in the castle.

There are a few dirty glasses in the sink, and the kettle is warm. I walk through to the Grand Hall where the long dining table has been set formally for brunch at ten o'clock.

The white linen tablecloth, gold-plated candelabras, and flower vases with freshly cut stocks, sunflowers and irises look resplendent in the early morning rays shining through the windows. The terrace doors are closed, so I walk around the table as if checking the place settings, rearranging a spoon, jug or fork, leaning over the table, knowing I'm about to take a considerable risk.

If Jim's cameras are trained on the table then I will be caught, but what alternative do I have?

I lean forward, stretching with my left hand to rearrange a yellow tulip while at the same time pulling the package with my right hand from my pocket. I slip the packet between the folds of the napkin.

It's over in a second.

I carry on walking around the table, one by one, to all the place settings and then I stand back and look at the table with a professional eye. It looks perfect. I turn my attention to the table against the wall. It's going to be a good day. Brunch. Champagne. Departure.

I'll make sure there's some food for later for the staff and me, or I'll pop into the local village pub this evening after they've all gone home.

I'm just pouring myself a coffee in the kitchen when Hugo and Mac arrive together. They seem to get on well, and they're sharing a joke, and I can't help but notice the difference between them. Although they're of a similar age, Mac is broad and rugged, whereby Hugo is slim but also muscular. In a contest, I'm not sure who would win.

'Ah, coffee.' Hugo smiles appreciatively.

'Morning.' I pour Hugo a mug. 'Mac, coffee?'

'I had one this morning already. Thanks.'

'You were up early.'

'Every morning.' He grins. 'I saw you jogging. You're very fit.'

Hugo looks surprised. 'Ronda jogging?' He turns to me. 'I thought you were joking when you said you went out early.'

'Thank you, Mac, my secret is out.' I poke out my tongue at Hugo. 'I have to keep fit for my kickboxing.'

Mac laughs. 'Was it you who kicked the stuffing out of Wilhelm last night?'

'Me? As if.'

'He wouldn't tell anyone. Jim was really annoyed. I had a feeling he was more embarrassed than hurt.' Mac's laugh is a deep rumble.

'What happened?' asks Hugo.

I don't reply, but I can't hide my smile of satisfaction.

'I think it had something to do with Freya, did it?' Mac guesses.

'Was it when you took the coffee upstairs?' Hugo looks concerned. 'Did Wilhelm hurt you?'

I shake my head. 'He was obnoxious and awful to Freya, so I left them alone, but after I took up the second coffee to Gunter on the terrace, he cornered me in the small hall. He said he wanted to talk, but he was drunk and vile.'

'So, you kicked him?' Hugo's face is a picture of incredulous admiration.

'He held me by the wrists. Look!' I pull up the sleeves of my whites and show them the bruising on my skin.

Both Mac and Hugo lean closely to look.

'That's not right.' Mac frowns. 'I'll tell—'

'No, please don't. It's best to say nothing. They're leaving at two o'clock and then it will all be over.'

'What time are you going?' Hugo asks.

'I'm staying until tomorrow morning. And you?' I ask.

'I'm taking the train tonight.'

The back door opens, and we all turn.

Julie appears, smiling. 'You'll never guess what's just happened?'

Chapter 13

'It's a bit embarrassing, really,' Julie says. 'I probably shouldn't say anything.'

'You have to tell us now,' I say.

'I've just seen Paula and Freya walking across the lawn toward the river. It looks like they're going for an early morning swim.'

'So, what's wrong with that?' Mac asks.

'They were holding hands,' Julie giggles. 'Who would have thought that amongst these arrogant and obnoxious guests, love would thrive?'

She reaches for her apron.

'There'll be some hangovers this morning, I'd imagine,' Mac says, hovering near Julie. I can see he's attracted to her. 'Some of them were still awake at three o'clock – drinking, up on the battlements. I brought some of the glasses down.' He nods at the sink.

'Thanks, Mac.' Julie beams at him.

'I'll have a quick wander around and see if there are any more glasses or food platters. It looked as if they ate the sandwiches I left out,' I say.

'I'll come with you.' Hugo places his mug on the counter and follows me outside, and whispers, 'We can leave the lovers to it.'

'Mac and Julie, do you think?'

'He's besotted with her.'

'You're such a gossip, Hugo.'

'I'm just interested.' We stop to survey the table in the Grand Hall. Hugo stands with his hands on his hips. 'It looks amazing.'

I smile. 'I think Mac did the flowers this morning.'

'Wow!'

'Let's go to the library and then up to the small hall,' I suggest, 'we can access the battlements that way, rather than through the towers and past the bedrooms. I'm sure most of the guests are still sleeping.' I want to see the spectacular sunrise, but I can't tell him that.

Hugo checks his watch.

'Six-thirty, the cleaners will be here shortly.'

We scan the library with the majestically book-lined walls, rich paintings, – not all originals – and ornaments and sculptures. We pick up a dirty ashtray, an empty brandy bottle and two glasses.

'One has lipstick on,' Hugo says raising the glass to the light.

'Paula and Freya?' I reply.

'Possibly.'

'No wonder Paula didn't join us in the kitchen for dinner. Come on, Inspector Clueless, let's go up to the small hall.'

I take my time to enjoy the quiet solitude of the small hall with the crossed swords on the wall, large tapestries and stained-glass windows. The sun begins to stream through the stained-glass leaving colourful patterns on the stone floor, and I'm absorbed in their hues and shapes.

'Do you like this room?' Hugo asks, standing behind me, looking down at the patterned floor.

I move around the room, stepping over the shapes of the colours dancing in the sunlight on the floor. Hugo moves with me, two metres apart, as if we're engaged in some ritual like a bullfighter or an Argentinian dance. 'I made a massive mistake; I trusted my boyfriend. He wanted me to invest in his business and, well basically, he took everything I had. He lied. He cheated me.'

'I'm sorry.' Hugo's voice is soft. 'What about the police?'

'I couldn't do that. I feel sorry for his mother. She's been so kind to me – it would kill her if anything happened to James.'

'Do you still see him?'

'He disappeared. I think he's changed his phone number.'

'That's terrible.'

'Worse still, Hugo. It damaged my confidence. I felt a failure for trusting him. I felt that my judgement was out of sync, then it turned out that I couldn't cook or do anything properly for months. I didn't trust myself. I didn't even want to go out of the house.'

'So, what did you do?'

'I went to the rescue centre.'

'Rescue?' He frowns.

I grin. 'I adopted a dog. It was all I could think of, and if I wouldn't go outside for me, then I would have to go out for Molly. I needed responsibility. So, I began taking her for long walks twice a day and, little by little, I'd speak to strangers –

other dog walkers – and then …' I clap my hands together. 'I began to make doggie treats; liver cakes and silly things like that … and then one morning, a few months ago, I finally wanted to cook again.'

I walk over to the window and gaze out at the chestnut and fir trees along the river bank.

'When Paula contacted me, I thought the job would be in London. I met Herr Schiltz in Canary Wharf, but not only was he the image of my father, he was also just as obnoxious. I couldn't believe it. I didn't want to take this job, but I had to.'

'You did the right thing.'

'I had to do it for me. I just never expected these awful people—' I pause thinking of the added complication of Inspector Joachin and the responsibility of what he's asked me to do '—to be so utterly vile.'

'Wilhelm has upset you?'

'He was drunk, he grabbed my hand and put it on his … you know, and I wasn't putting up with that. I might have hit him a bit hard. I took out my frustration on him.'

Hugo laughs. 'He'll be fine. It's the embarrassment he'll have to live with.'

I don't tell him about my kickboxing skills; it will seem like I'm bragging.

'Look!' I point out of the window. 'Look, there's Freya. She's lovely, but they're all so complicated. She's in love with Paula.'

Hugo joins me at the window, and we watch them running naked across the grass toward the house. They're carrying their clothes, they have wet hair, and they're laughing.

'Ah, true love.' He smiles. 'There's nothing like it.'

'Rubbish! Let's just finish this job and go home.'

He reaches out for my hand, but I pull away from him and

shake my head.

'I just want to get back to Molly.'

* * *

It's mid-morning, the kitchen is busy, bustling, and Hugo is taking orders from the family as they gather at the table.

Julie has squeezed fresh grapefruit and oranges, Mrs Long is cooking bacon, and I have the kippers simmering while I prepare the kedgeree.

Paula comes in looking flustered and tired as if she hasn't slept.

'There's coffee on the range, help yourself.' I nod at the coffee pot, smiling. 'There are warm croissants in the oven or, if you wait a few minutes, we can make you something more substantial.'

'It's fine. Don't worry about me. I came in here to escape,' she whispers.

'From who?' I ask.

'This weekend has been a nightmare,' she says. 'I can generally deal with Herr Schiltz, but the rest of his family have been positively hostile toward me.'

'Well, not for much longer. Are they all downstairs yet?'

'Not Herr and Frau Schiltz. They're coming in last so that the family will applaud Louisa. As it's the last morning, he'd like all the kitchen staff and everyone to be present too, to clap her in as she comes down the stairs.'

'Oh, great,' I mutter then I say more loudly, 'Check with Mrs Long and she will tell all the staff.'

'Be careful this morning, Ronda. Wilhelm is hungover and angry. He has the most awful bruised cheek. He's so rude – he even pushed me out of the way, I almost fell down the stairs.'

'Can you stay away from him?' I suggest.

'It's difficult when you meet each other on the narrow staircase.'

'That's true.' As bad as my weekend has been, it must be nothing compared to what Paula has gone through. 'Where's Jim? 'I ask.'

'I don't know. I haven't seen him this morning.'

'Can you take some time off for a holiday?'

'I don't know what will happen. Now that Herr Schiltz is resigning, I guess my job will go too.'

'Can you work for Gunter, if he's relocating to London?'

Paula shrugs. 'He has his own staff, and personal secretary, maybe she will move to London, too.'

'Don't worry, Paula. It will all get sorted out. Give it time.'

She moves away to speak to Mrs Long, and meanwhile, I check the guests' orders. I begin to prepare the Eggs Benedict.

Ten minutes later, Dan comes in and announces, 'Mrs Long wants us all in the Grand Hall. Frau Schiltz is expected down shortly.'

Julie and I swap an annoyed look of resignation.

I rinse my hands quickly under the tap, dry my small santoku knife and file out of the kitchen and into the Grand Hall.

The family are standing behind their chairs. The only vacant chairs are at each end of the long table.

Above us in the gallery a door slams, then Herr and Frau Schiltz appear from the tower at the far end. They walk regally along the gallery corridor looking down at us below. Louisa acts surprised then raises her hand to wave. Below, Fran and Mike begin the applause enthusiastically.

Louisa wears a red and gold summer dress, and her tanned

skin and bleached hair give her face a look of someone who loves the outdoors, being on the golf course. She's holding her husband's arm, smiling and looking radiant. The family and staff are all clapping. Jack includes a *whoop whoop* for his mother while Freya and Paula share a shy smile.

Roma claps enthusiastically, and only Wilhelm tugs at his shirt and pretends nothing extraordinary is happening.

Beside me, Mac claps slowly looking bored, and Julie grins excitedly. The only person missing is Jim.

Louisa and Herr Schiltz saunter down the grand staircase and she exclaims her delight with everyone as if she's surprised they are all there. It's a marvellous act, and I suppress a giggle, but then Julie looks at me, and we burst out laughing.

The happy couple reaches the lower step, the applause increases and Mac whistles. Herr Schiltz leads his wife to the top of the table.

I freeze.

Herr Schiltz pulls out the chair for his wife.

I placed the package at the wrong end. Because he sat on the right last night, I assumed he'd sit there this morning, but he's deliberately walked her past the family.

The package is now under her napkin.

I hold my breath.

I've made a mistake, I've let Inspector Joachin down. Suddenly I feel incapable again. I'm useless. My newfound confidence freezes as the applause dies.

'Thank you, thank you. What a lovely greeting this morning.' Louisa waves for them all to be seated then she turns her attention to us, the humble staff lined up like we're in an old-fashioned movie. 'Thank you all. You've made a magnificent job of everything. We've had a lovely weekend. I'm sure all the family, like me, are *simply starving.*'

That earns a ripple of laughter.

That's our cue to leave, and I'm the first to move.

In the kitchen, I don't look up as I prepare breakfast. I call to Hugo and Dan to carry it out, but then I take out Herr and Frau Schiltz's breakfast personally.

I retie my bandana, pull down my tunic, and carry the kippers into the Grand Hall.

I place his breakfast on the table, and Dan and Hugo serve the family. Finally, I put Louisa's breakfast in front of her.

'Oh, Ronda. This looks simply delicious. Thank you.'

'You're welcome, Mrs Schiltz.' I can't help but glance at the linen napkin, and I freeze as Louisa reaches out and the package is revealed.

'Oh, my goodness, what's this?' she says excitedly, looking down the table at her family.

I step away.

Herr Schiltz and Hugo look up, and Dan disappears.

The family are all focused on Louisa's excited expression.

I back away, slowly, toward the kitchen door, and I feel Hugo at my side.

Louisa is waving the package. 'How exciting! Is this for me? A late birthday present?'

Herr Schiltz looks bemused and shrugs.

'It's obviously not from your husband,' Fran calls unnecessarily.

'It must be a surprise,' Freya says, sitting beside her mother, looking interested.

'Okay, so which one of you has been busy buying me another gift? Oh, how lovely!'

'It's a shame about the paper,' Jack calls. He's on the other side of his mother but speaks loud enough for everyone to hear. 'Whoever it was could have made more of an effort.'

'Oh, don't be silly, it's only a bit of packaging.' Louisa uses her knife to slide under the envelope flap. She peers inside and frowns. 'What's this?'

She tilts it, and the object slides easily into her hand.

It's a Smith & Wesson revolver. The gun clatters onto her plate and into her kedgeree.

* * *

'Oh, my God,' I whisper.

'Quickly. Get in the kitchen.' Hugo pushes me in the back. I stumble, but quickly regain my balance.

Mrs Long is at the door. 'What's happened?' she asks.

'I don't know,' I stammer.

Hugo says, 'There's a problem.'

'With the food?' Mrs Long looks aghast.

'No.' He turns back to look through the kitchen door, and Mrs Long pushes past me to look with him. Through the gap over their shoulders, Herr Schiltz has moved quickly to his wife's side at the head of the table.

Jack has also stood up and is leaning over his mother. Freya has moved away, obviously upset.

Herr Schiltz stares down at the gun lying on the kipper kedgeree and very carefully pulls it out with two fingers. He picks up the discarded napkin and wraps up the weapon, then he looks around the table, his eyes burning furiously.

'Is this someone's idea of a joke?' He looks icily around the room. 'Well?'

Jack says, 'It's a gun.'

'I know it's a gun!' He turns angrily on his stepson. 'Who put it here?'

'Why would someone do that?' asks Fran.

'Who put this here?' Herr Schiltz demands. 'No one is leaving this room until I have some answers.'

'What sort of gun is it?' asks Mike, struggling to his feet but Fran pulls on his arm to make him sit back down.

'Does it matter?' Herr Schiltz replies.

'If it's a Smith & Wesson, it might.' Mike stands up.

Fran gasps.

Louisa covers her face with her hands while Jack stands protectively behind her with his arm across her shoulder.

The room is hushed.

Mike walks to the head of the table, and Herr Schiltz obligingly unfolds the napkin. They look at each other.

'I think we should call the police,' Freya says.

'Oh, no. We'll never get out of here,' Wilhelm cries. 'We'll never get home.'

'That's not appropriate,' his father admonishes him.

Mrs Long whispers, 'Shall I call the police?'

'Let's wait and see, Mrs Long.' Hugo places a reassuring hand on her arm.

'Why is it important if it's a Smith & Wesson?' asks Roma. No one replies, so she says,' If you want the truth, Friedrich, then you have to be honest and tell us. Unless it's, oh no …'

Gunter says, 'Stop it, Roma.'

Louisa buries her head in her son's waist while Herr Schiltz carries the weapon to the opposite end of the table.

'Their breakfast is getting cold,' whispers Mrs Long.

Hugo and I ignore her.

'Right,' Herr Schiltz says decisively. 'I don't know what

you're playing at, whoever you are, so we'll put this aside, we'll eat our breakfast and carry on.'

'Is that the gun?' Gunter shouts. 'The gun that killed our mother?'

Herr Schiltz looks down at the napkin. 'I don't know.'

'Is it the same make and model?' Gunter moves quickly to his father's side. 'It is. Tell me the truth.'

'Yes.' Herr Schiltz's voice is hoarse. 'Yes. I believe it is.'

* * *

Beside me, Mrs Long gasps at the same time as the commotion breaks out in the Grand Hall and I feel Hugo's body tense.

'Give it to me!'

'I want to see it!'

'Don't be ridiculous!'

'Who put it there?'

'How did it get there?'

'Where's Jim?'

'Mum was killed five years ago!'

'Who knows about this?'

'Where has the gun been?'

'Tell Paula to call the police.'

'Iris was shot dead!'

'They caught the killer!'

'Don't be stupid. He was the gardener.'

'He had an alibi.'

'They paid off—'

Herr Schiltz bellows,' Someone here, knows all about it! One of you put it here deliberately.'

It's Paula who then steps forward and says quietly, 'With

great respect, Herr Schiltz. I think a brief explanation is needed, and then we need to call the police.'

'Jim?' Herr Schiltz shouts, ignoring her. 'Jim!'

Gunter stands beside his father. 'Give me the gun. I'm not letting it out of my sight. We can find the bastard who killed her once and for all.' He holds out his hand, but Herr Schiltz won't part with it.

'Sit down, Gunter.'

'Let me have it,' says Mike.

'Put it away,' cries Fran.

'Whoever put it here knows all about it. It was one of you,' Jack shouts. 'It was somebody here – one of the family.'

'Not necessarily.' Wilhelm turns to the kitchen. 'It might have been put here by someone else.'

Mrs Long, Hugo and I back away from the door.

'We need to call the police,' Mrs Long whispers. 'I've never seen anything like this.'

Chapter 14

'Death and genitals are things that frighten people, and when people are frightened, they develop means of concealment and aggression. It is common sense.'
Noam Chomsky

I stare out of the kitchen window; on the wall Bobby the blackbird sings then stops suddenly to peck at his wing before resuming his song. In his world nothing has changed, but I fear mine has come tumbling down around me.

Inspector Joachin left me the package to place at Herr Schiltz's plate, and now it's been a disaster. He knew the gun was inside. He did it deliberately. Is this the gun that killed Iris Schiltz?

Is this what Inspector Joachin wanted?

'Ronda? What's happened?' Julie asks, coming to stand beside me. 'Are you alright?'

'I don't know.'

I can't tell her that this is all my fault and that I was the one who left the package on the table.

What if they call the police?

'Ronda? Are you alright?' Julie insists.

'They've got a gun,' Dan says. He's standing near the door,

eavesdropping on the scene in the Grand Hall, but I can't bear to look.

If this is the gun that killed Iris Schiltz, then who put it under my bed?

'I'm not going in there again.' Dan picks up a tea towel. 'They're all nuts. He shouldn't have a weapon.'

'Is it loaded?' asks Julie, removing her apron. 'Where's Mac?'

'He was here a minute ago,' Dan says, looking around.

'Go and find him,' Julie orders.

Mrs Long is now sitting at the kitchen table looking flustered and hot as if she's about to have a heart attack.

'You'd better make her a cup of tea,' I say to Dan, trying to rally myself, but what can I do, apart from wait and see how it all plays out.

Julie says again. 'Dan, go and find Mac.'

'What shall we do about breakfast?' Mrs Long wails.

'We'll have to wait until things calm down,' I reply.

The door opens. Hugo and Julie back away as Mike comes into the kitchen.

'Everyone and I mean everyone, in the Grand Hall, *now!*'

* * *

Mike, Herr Schiltz's business partner, takes control. He ushers us inside the big room. The staff stand together, near the wall where we displayed the birthday cake yesterday: Hugo, Julie, Dan, Mrs Long, the cleaner and her sister, and me.

Mac must have heard the commotion, and he comes in via the kitchen and heads straight to Herr Schiltz.

'I'm the estate manager, and I'm responsible for Castle Calder. I want to inspect the weapon, please.'

Herr Schiltz looks as if he might argue, but then he hands the gun to Mac.

Mac appears to inspect it thoroughly, and when he hands it back, he announces,

'The gun isn't loaded, but I'd appreciate you leaving it on the table in full sight of everyone until the police arrive.'

'I'll decide what I'll do, and if we're calling the police. Just give me a minute.' Herr Schiltz places the gun carefully on the table.

Jim walks in from the terrace. His bulky frame blocks the sunlight from the open doors, but he stands menacingly as if he's there to stop anyone from running into the garden.

'Return to your seats.' Herr Schiltz stands at the head of the table, and he indicates Paula to stand with him, with her clipboard.

She looks terrified.

Louisa is sitting in her seat, gazing at the floor. Jack sits protectively beside her with his arm on the back of her chair, and Freya looks shocked and makes no attempt to speak.

Subconsciously I move closer to Hugo. He takes my fingers in his and squeezes them quickly before releasing my hand.

Herr Schiltz clears his throat.

'This was to have been an extraordinary weekend, not only for Louisa, as it's her birthday, but for all of us – family and friends together. I have deliberately given a great deal of thought, as I told you yesterday, to our future and my retirement. One that Louisa and I were looking forward to with excitement. But this has changed everything. So, I hope – whoever planted this here, whoever has been keeping this for the past few years – that you are very proud of yourselves.'

He strokes his moustache before composing himself.

'If you wanted to ruin the weekend, then you have achieved your goal. However, in presenting this, this weapon in such an obvious way – it will no doubt, as you have anticipated, cause a great deal of distress to us both, to us all, including Gunter and Wilhelm our two sons. Now, my first question is, who had this gun?' He looks slowly around the table, making eye contact with everyone. 'I know it's the same model that killed Iris, five years ago, but is it the same gun or a replica?'

He coughs and appears to control himself before he continues.

'I must hand it to the police, and I shall do that. But, I'd like to give the person a chance to come forward first. You are my family and friends. I give you the courtesy you deserve. I will help and protect you as much as the law will allow me to.'

He turns to us. His eyes are hard and cold.

'You are all members of staff here at Castle Calder. You have been chosen to work with us this weekend and I will extend the same courtesy to you. If, for whatever reason, you know anything about this, then I suggest you come clean. Tell the truth, and I will help you.'

Herr Schiltz clears his throat and continues, looking back at his family.

'I've had this castle under surveillance the whole time we've been here. Jim placed cameras in most of the rooms, and throughout the grounds. I'm confident that once we have looked at them all, the evidence will be clear. I will see who placed the gun inside Louisa's napkin. So, I'd advise you to be truthful now. Step forward, and we can discuss this in private.'

No one moves.

'Right.' He looks over to us, and I feel his eyes burning into me. 'Take this cold breakfast away. Serve coffee and bring something else for us to eat. This is all ruined.' He checks his watch. 'It's eleven o'clock now, and the minibus leaves at two o'clock. We will continue this brunch as if nothing has happened – but I warn you, *I will find you.* You will not get away with this.'

He nods at Jim who nods back.

'Once we have the video and the evidence – it will be solved.'

Herr Schiltz smiles, reminding me once again of my dead departed father when I was seven. He dug a hole in the garden for my pet rabbit and he grinned and said, 'Lucky for Fiver, that he's not ending up in the boiling pot!'

* * *

I'm shaking, trying to control my nerves and angry at my body's reaction. I want to be stronger than this. I need to be tougher. I'm trying to focus on what to serve the guests as Dan and Hugo return with untouched breakfasts.

Tempers are short.

'Dan,' shouts Mrs Long. 'Clean those plates. Julie, sort the drinks, tea, coffee and juices. Find me some more bacon.'

Dan complains when Julie bumps him, and he spills fresh orange juice on the floor. Then he burns his hand in hot water.

Mrs Long barks instructions, taking over the kitchen as if it's what this castle had needed all along while I begin mixing scrambled eggs. I can't speak, I can't look up, and my hands are shaking.

Mrs Long issues instructions to Dan for more toast.

Outside, I pick fresh chives from the garden, and the scent of the herbs calms me momentarily; mint, rosemary, thyme. Bobby the blackbird watches me then his yellow beak begins pecking at the wooden fence.

I want to run. I could go back to my room, grab my bag and leave. Get the train to London and disappear.

'Ronda? Are you alright?'

'Hello, Mac, it's all been a shock, and it's thrown me, I don't know what to cook, but your mother, um … Mrs Long is amazing.'

He grins. 'She always rallies when there's a disaster. She's good in a crisis.'

'I used to be,' I grumble.

'Don't worry.'

'What will happen now?'

'Two o'clock can't come fast enough. I can't wait for them to go,' he says.

I'm afraid to linger outside, and he follows me into the kitchen.

'Mac,' says Mrs Long. 'Go inside there and tell them that as estate manager, you want to lock the gun away.'

'There are no bullets in it. Mr Schiltz and I looked at it together. No one is in any danger.'

'What if they've got other bullets?' she asks.

'He's promised to leave it in full sight of everyone.'

He turns his back to her, and so I ask him, 'What do you make of all this?'

'I guess we should call the police, but nothing has happened. We don't know it's the actual murder weapon that was used to kill his first wife, and I guess that by the time Jim's looked at the cameras they've hidden in the Grand Hall, they'll know which one of them put it there.'

My hands tremble. I can take on one of them, but I couldn't face the wrath of Herr Schiltz.

'To be honest, Ronda. I don't care. They can all piss off and leave us be.' He grins and walks off, leaving me shaking and feeling as though I'm going to be sick outside, all over the herb garden.

* * *

We finish making eggs and bacon, Dan and Hugo deliver the plates to the tables, and I don't venture back inside the hall. They report back that everyone is eating, but Mrs Long goes to double-check.

'What will they all be talking about in there? It's hardly a celebration weekend now, is it?' Dan says.

'I wonder who put the gun there,' Julie says. 'It seems a strange thing to do, don't you think?'

'What do you think, Ronda?' Dan asks.

I shake my head. 'I don't know what to think.'

'You've gone very pale.' Julie grins.

'What if it's the revolver that was used to kill someone?' Dan asks.

'We don't know that.' Julie folds her arms.

Mrs Long reappears and sinks dramatically into a seat and leans on the table. 'My heart can't take much more. Herr Schiltz is furious and I don't blame him. He's gone to all this trouble to make it a lovely weekend for his family and look what they've done.'

'Who do you think put it there?' Dan chirps. 'I'd hate to get on the wrong side of Jim.'

'My money is on the nerd that caused all the trouble yesterday.' Dan wipes the counter.

'You think it's Wilhelm?' asks Julie. 'But it was his mum who died. He wouldn't kill his mother, would he?'

'You wouldn't know with that lot, 'Dan replies. 'I overheard the older brother talking yesterday, Gunter. He doesn't like Louisa. He blames her for his mother's death. He said that Louisa and randy Friedrich had been having an affair for years before his wife died—'

'Dan!' Julie scolds him. 'That's not nice.'

'Well, it's true. Someone killed her, and if that's the gun that did it, then—'

A small groan escapes Mrs Long's lips. She looks pale and worried.

'What's wrong?' Julie asks her.

Mrs Long shakes her head. 'I shouldn't say.'

'Oh, come on. We're all in this together.' Julie rubs her arm. 'I'll get you some tea, tell us.'

'I only went out to make sure that Mrs Schiltz, Louisa, was alright. But it's the way they are all talking. They're all accusing each other. Presumably, the gun has been missing since the day the first Mrs Schiltz was murdered. The police never found the murder weapon at the scene of the crime.'

'So, the family think this is the real one?' Dan asks.

'Herr Schiltz seems to think so, but then he's confused. On the one hand, he keeps saying it's impossible, then on the other, he's trying to find out how anyone could have it in their possession – almost as if—' She stops abruptly.

'Almost as if what?' Julie prompts her and places strong tea on the table.

'Almost as if he, as if *he* knew where it was …'

'That's not possible, is it?' Dan asks. 'Unless he killed his own wife.'

'He didn't kill her,' Mrs Long says.' He said something about a river bursting its banks. He's not making any sense at all.'

I lean against the kitchen sink with a sick feeling of understanding.

Inspector Joachin had said that someone shot Iris Schiltz. He also said the murder weapon was missing. I'm trying to remember the details of what he told us in the London pub. The riverbank had broken. It swept away several buildings, including the foundations of a bank where Herr Schiltz had kept many valuable items. On the insurance claim, he'd initially said there were nine items and then changed his mind when only eight were found. What if he had kept the gun that killed his wife in the safety deposit box? What if the weapon had been swept away, along with the bank's foundations, in the storm?

Now, it's turned up on the dining table in Castle Calder, Scotland.

That would be a shock to him.

I stare out of the kitchen window. The German police must have found it. Inspector Joachin told me to put it in front of Herr Schiltz but why?

What was the motive?

Why not just arrest Herr Schiltz?

Hugo comes into the kitchen, carrying an empty bottle of champagne.

'Don't tell me they're drinking alcohol?' Mrs Long sounds shocked.

'They're determined to enjoy Mrs Schiltz's birthday weekend, but everything is about to get interesting.' Hugo holds my gaze. 'Jim is back, and he's smiling. He must have found someone on the camera.'

CHAPTER 14

* * *

'Hugo,' I whisper urgently, once we're out of earshot of the other staff. 'I need your help.'

He smiles at me. 'Anytime, my fair lady.'

'I want to see what's going on in the Grand Hall. Didn't you say there was another secret passage?'

'Not one that spies on the Grand Hall.'

I shake my head and frown. How else was I going to be forewarned?

Hugo smiles. 'But there is a hiding place on the inner corridor where we can watch. Come on.'

I follow him up the back stairs into the inner corridor leading around the top of the Grand Hall. He puts a finger to his lips, and we tiptoe and hide alongside a hand-carved, oak chest.

We're at the side of the Grand Hall, above the terrace doors, peering through the crafted wooden railing at the big table downstairs.

Jim is leaning over the shoulder of his employer, showing him his phone and camera. Herr Schiltz watches with interest and then tosses his napkin aside.

The conversation around the table dies as the group wait. Louisa sits up in her chair, watching with interest and Jack looks as though he'd like to kill someone.

'Well, this is interesting,' Herr Schiltz announces.

Hugo squeezes my hand, and I press back, reassured that he's with me. I exhale quietly.

'We know,' Herr Schiltz announces. 'We know who did it. We have it on camera.'

Jim stands proudly at his side.

165

I hold my breath. They're going to come looking for me, and I won't be there. I'll ask Hugo to smuggle me out, but then they know about these secret hiding places, and they will find me and they'll—

'Who put it there?' demands Gunter.

Herr Schiltz holds up his hand and addresses the table.

'This is your opportunity. I want you to do the responsible and honourable thing. This is a test,' he announces. 'And, your inheritance will be dependent on the outcome today. You have until one o'clock to come forward, or you won't be getting on the minibus to come with us to the airport. You'll be going to a Scottish prison to await extradition to go on trial in Germany for the murder of my wife – Iris Schiltz – five years ago.'

I slump against Hugo.

They can't know it's me. He can't have seen me put the package under the napkin. Herr Schiltz and Jim must be lying, but why?

'Now, in the meantime, we're going to have champagne, toast my wife and finish this birthday weekend in style. Would anyone like more birthday cake, from yesterday?'

'Shit!' I whisper.

Hugo pushes me ahead of him, and we crouch running down the steps and fall into the pantry, tripping over each other.

'Sorry, Ronda! He'll be looking for me to serve the cham-pagne.'

My heart thumping, my head is trying to make sense of what's happening. He'll be looking for me too. I'd forgotten about the bloody cake!

Chapter 15

'Big companies are like marching bands. Even if half the band is playing random notes, it still sounds kind of like music. The concealment of failure is built into them.'
Douglas Coupland

After drinking champagne and eating birthday cake, the guests begin to disperse up to their rooms to pack their weekend bags, and some, according to Hugo, go upstairs and take a final look from the battlements.

I take this opportunity to escape back to my room. If Inspector Joachin managed to get into my room to put the package in there last night, he must be nearby. More importantly, if he got into my room – then so could Jim.

I must tell him I'm in danger.

I'm worried that when the family meet up, I will be hauled out in front of them all and held to account for leaving the gun, in the package, on the table.

I walk quickly, fumble for my key and enter my room. The bed is still unmade, and my dirty whites from yesterday are slung in the corner on the floor.

I rummage in my bag with shaking hands looking for Inspector Joachin's phone.

There's one message. He sent it at midday – an hour ago.

Thanks for your help, Ronda. All is going well.

I type.

I'm glad you think so! I'm terrified. They have a picture of me leaving the package on the table. If I get caught – what will I do?

After deleting the message, I sit on the bed waiting, but there's no answer.

I brush my teeth, fix my bandana, and in the end, I stow the mobile under my bed.

As I'm locking the door, a hand from behind me covers my mouth, and someone yanks my right hand up behind my back.

I react instinctively, twisting and bending forward with all my strength and then I'm spinning, kicking and biting, keeping the momentum and holding his arm as I bend over and haul him over my shoulders. He loosens his grip, and I kick out with my sneakers, missing his balls, but kicking him in the lower stomach. Wilhelm doubles over gasping for breath.

He groans. I'm furious.

I step back and rotating my torso I bring my fist upward, striking him on the chin. I hop from foot to foot, getting my fists to my face in a fighting stance waiting for Wilhelm to look up but he doesn't. Instead, he charges blindly at me in a rugby tackle.

I shift my weight to my right foot and bring my left knee up to my chest, and I kick out my left foot – straight from the hip – leading with the heel smacking him in the shoulder, and he sprawls at my feet.

I bring my foot to the middle of his back and push down hard. Then I retain my fighting stance over his body on the ground.

'Do you want more? You snivelling little creep?'

Wilhelm groans and sits up. He leans his arms on his knees and shakes his head. 'I wanted to teach you a lesson but—'

'Why?'

'You made me look stupid last night.'

'You didn't need my help with that.'

He shakes his head in defeat. His cheek is swollen and bruised. He stands up slowly brushing the dust off his trousers. I don't help him.

'It's been a shitty weekend. I'm sorry, Ronda. I guess I took it out on you.'

I haven't let down my fighting guard. I'm ready in case he charges me again.

'Friends?' He holds out his hand.

'Never.'

He looks surprised. 'Okay, I can understand that. I haven't behaved well. But this whole charade this weekend has been awful. Do you have any idea what it's like watching your father make a fool of himself over that woman? He's been doing it for years, with no regard for Gunter or me or even for our mother. He was sleeping with Louisa before our mother died.'

He rubs his head. His eyes are bloodshot, and he looks like he has a stinking hangover.

'They were having an affair, and we all knew it. Including our mother. It's humiliating and now, having to come here this weekend and pretend that we like her and her two children is beyond my limits.'

He turns away to look at the chestnuts and firs in the distance, and it gives me a chance to study his profile, his swollen bruised eye and his clenching jaw.

'Mike emailed me. He told me he wanted to expand the company. He's been wanting to do it for years, importing and exporting to and from America, but Dad's always resisted, America never interested him. He's a control freak and America, and expansion frightens him. He's lost his edge. He was a good businessman, but he's lost it. He's only got eyes for her. She controls him.'

'I don't believe that.' I'm still in my boxing stance.

'No, well, what would you know? You're only a cook.' He turns away and calls over his shoulder, 'And a mediocre one at that.'

I'm inclined to run at him, kick him in the back of the calf and break his bones but I don't. He has to get over his second bout of humiliation, so I'll let him have that point.

I find the key to my room on the floor. I pick it up and lock it securely, and then I walk back to the main house with my chest thumping. 'Half an hour,' I say to Bobby the blackbird twittering on the garden fence. 'Then they are all gone.'

* * *

Paula gives me instructions that the cake and extra food are to be packed up, and it keeps me busy. Hugo is placing the uncorked bottles in the crates and I assume he'll carry them to the Mercedes that Jim drove up in from London.

I feel my mood lifting, knowing they will soon be gone, and beside me Julie is humming as we clean and pack up together.

Only Mrs Long is unhappy. 'There's still the matter of that gun,' she complains. 'We need to call the police.'

'They'll be leaving soon,' Julie says.

'Thank goodness. My back is killing me. I can't wait to get home and put my feet up. I'm exhausted.'

'Only a little while, Mrs Long. You can go home early after

the guests have gone. Ronda and I can finish up.'

'You're a good girl, Julie. Thank you.'

'They're gathering in the Grand Hall,' Dan says. 'It looks as if they can't wait to leave here either. Is the minibus here yet? I'm going away tonight for our friends stag weekend in Belgium, and I'm not missing that flight for anything.'

'Hugo? What time is your train?' Mrs Long asks.

'At six o'clock.'

'Mac will take you to the station.'

'Great. Thank you.' Hugo heads out of the kitchen towards the cellar.

'You'll be on your own here tonight, Ronda,' Mrs Long says. 'But Mac will be around if you need anything.'

'I'll be fine. I'll take a walk and sleep. Don't worry about me. I might even try the village pub.'

'Herr Schiltz is speaking to the family,' Dan whispers, standing at the door to the Grand Hall. 'Do you want to listen?'

They all crowd at the door, but I hang back, waiting and wondering if Jim will come and get me. I hear Herr Schiltz's voice above the hum of the dishwasher and Bobby the blackbird singing outside on the fence.

I hardly dare to breathe.

Herr Schiltz's voice is measured and calm.

'This has been an interesting weekend, and I've given the events some thought. As you know, I wanted to tell you in person that I was resigning from my position on the board, and as managing director. I also wanted to discuss the future of the ongoing business with my sons who have, under the circumstances, been very understanding.'

I leave the kitchen table and wander to the doorway to look over Julie's shoulder at the family.

There hasn't been a mention of Louisa or her birthday weekend.

Herr Schiltz is holding court at the head of the table. There's no sign of Jim or Paula.

Herr Schiltz nods at his lawyer. 'Paula will liaise with the lawyers and make the necessary adjustments to the company paperwork. Mike and I will sort out the business details. Thank you all for coming here and for taking the time to celebrate Louisa's birthday – I'm sure you'll all agree, it's been a weekend we will all remember.'

There are smiles of appreciation and a small clap from Roma and Fran.

'Unfortunately, there's one detail that's hanging over our heads. That's the matter of the parcel left for Louisa, but then I began to wonder if the parcel was meant for me? You see, that's where I sat last night and no one knew – not even me – that I would exchange seats. So, knowing that this wasn't directed at Louisa but rather at me, I will consider this after the weekend is over – and notify the police.'

'Good,' Fran shouts. 'You know Iris and I were the best of friends. That's not to say, I don't love you, Louisa – but it's the right thing to do, Friedrich.'

'Thank you, Fran.' Herr Schiltz bows his head in acknowledgement. 'However, I feel that certain questions still need to be answered. So, I have asked Paula…' He pauses, and everyone looks around for her, but she isn't in the room. 'To arrange for us to stay on for one more night.'

In the kitchen, Mrs Long lets out a short gasp.

'What?' cries Dan.

'No shit,' adds Julie.

A small groan breaks out in the Grand Hall, but Herr Schiltz holds up his hand.

'Not all of you will stay. Some of you will be going home. Louisa and I will stay, as will Fran and Mike, and Gunter and Roma. Just the six of us.'

Roma looks positively upset.

'I can't stay. The children need me. I must—'

'Paula is arranging everything. It will all be sorted out in a few more minutes.'

'Am I staying?' Wilhelm calls.

'No. You're not required.'

Wilhelm looks furious. 'But we can stay. Chloe and I can stay. We don't have to get back to—'

'No, thank you, Wilhelm. You are going home. There are just six of us staying. I'm rather hoping we can persuade some of the kitchen staff to stay on too.'

We all move back from the door, hoping they won't see us, but knowing they have.

'I'm not staying,' Dan whispers.

'I can't do any more. I'll be ill with my heart.' Mrs Long looks visibly distraught, and Julie takes her hands.

'It's alright, Mrs Long. I can stay. I'll do one more night and Ronda is here anyway, aren't you?'

I pause. I can't refuse. 'Of course.'

'There's only six of them and two of us. It will be like cooking dinner at home, won't it, Ronda?'

I'm thinking of the implications. It isn't just the number of people to cater for because there's also Jim and Paula.

I'm more concerned that this is Herr Schiltz's way of getting me on my own.

Is he getting rid of everyone so I am here, at their mercy?

'Are you wondering what to cook, Ronda?' Dan grins.

'You look like the judge has just given you a life sentence for murder.'

* * *

We're expected to wait outside Castle Calder, as is tradition, and wave off the guests. We line up as if it's a Downton Abbey send-off. Mrs Long, Julie, Dan, and the cleaner and her sister and me with Hugo and Mac at the end of the line.

Herr Schiltz and the remaining guests wait at the bottom of the steps, near the minibus that will take the others to the airport.

Freya kisses me on the cheeks and whispers, 'Thanks, Ronda.'

'I'm pleased it's all worked out.'

'You know?' She sounds surprised and frowns at me. 'Is it that obvious?'

'Well aside from you looking much happier, I saw you both running back from the river this morning.'

Freya giggles and I realise she's a pretty young girl and I imagine how Louisa, her mother, must have looked in her twenties.

I smile. 'Good luck.'

'We'll need it.'

'I'd love another night here. Louisa is so lucky to have such a thoughtful and wonderful husband,' Chloe says loudly. 'Thank you, Ronda. Superb food.'

Jack hugs his mother and walks past me without saying a word.

Wilhelm follows him; he doesn't look at me, and I get a flicker of satisfaction when I glimpse his bruised cheek.

Chloe stops in front of me.

'Thank you, Ronda.'

'You're welcome.'

She leans closer to me and drawls, 'It was very unnecessary what you did to Wilhelm yesterday. He was drunk. He didn't deserve that.'

'Chloe, get on the bus,' Wilhelm shouts from his seat on the bus.

'One day you'll get your comeuppance,' she whispers. 'And it might be quite soon.'

* * *

Paula is waiting in the kitchen with her clipboard.

'Please can I ask for your help, Ronda?' She looks earnestly at me. 'Herr Schiltz will pay you well for this extra day. The same as for the entire weekend. Paid directly into your bank account first thing in the morning.'

'Of course.' I smile. I am pleased with the thought of the extra money.

'I've checked with the reservation company, and they are happy to extend the stay for one night. They've been in touch with Mac, and he's also happy with the arrangement.'

'The guests have gone.' Hugo comes into the kitchen. 'Herr Schiltz and Louisa are taking a walk to the river. Fran and Mike have retired to their rooms and Gunter and Roma would like coffee on the battlements.'

'Where's the gun?' asks Julie.

Mac replies, 'I have it locked away. It was one of the conditions that I let them stay, but to be honest, I don't think anyone has any bullets. Someone produced it for effect. To shock.'

'It certainly did that!' Mrs Long says.

'Who will make the coffee?' Hugo looks at Julie and smiles.

Julie moves to the kettle. 'I'll do it.'

Mac watches her walk across the kitchen, but she won't meet his gaze. She ignores him.

'Jim and I are also staying,' Paula adds.' Is that alright? Will there be plenty of food?'

'I can always go into town,' Mac replies.

'Can I go now?' Dan asks Mrs Long. 'I've got a flight to catch this evening.'

'Of course, I'll be leaving shortly. I've told Mr Schiltz that you'll be cooking tonight, Ronda, and you'll be serving the table, Julie.'

A small giggle escapes Julie's lips.

Mac grins and looks at me. 'So, it's all worked out. The six guests can eat in the Grand Hall, and the six workers can eat down here.'

I count them in my head: Mac, Julie, Jim, Paula and me. 'Six?'

'Hugo has cancelled his train. He's leaving tomorrow now.'

My tummy flutters momentarily, blocking out the fear that Jim has a recording of me placing the package on the table.

What are they planning?

I must take care.

I pull out my notepad and pencil.

'What are you doing?' asks Mac.

'I'm going to have a coffee and plan the dinner menu, is that okay?'

'Your hands are shaking badly, Ronda. Are you sure you're alright?'

* * *

My hands are still shaking when I let myself into my room an hour later. I fumble for my phone, expecting a long message from Inspector Joachin explaining how he will rescue me.

I pull out the phone he gave me, but there's no message. There's no reply from Inspector Joachin.

I type:

I'm worried. 6 guests and Hugo staying an extra night. Herr S has the gun. Help!

I send then delete the message.

* * *

After saying farewell to Mrs Long, the afternoon is quiet. We prepare what we can for dinner, and afterwards Julie and I agree to some free time to relax which seems ambitious considering how wired and anxious I am. When I look out of the kitchen window, Bobby is tweeting happily, his world unchanged.

Julie disappears around the corner of the secret herb garden without a backward glance where I assume she'll sit in the sunshine and smoke a cigarette.

I'm making tea when Hugo walks in.

'Is there enough in the pot for me?'

'Where have you been?'

'Checking on things.'

'Like what?'

He grins mysteriously. 'Things.'

'Do you want to sit outside with me or are you busy?'

'No, I'm all yours.'

'You wish,' I quip and carry our mugs outside.

There's no sign of Julie, and we sit companionably on the bench in the afternoon sunshine.

'Well, that was an unusual weekend …' I say. 'How come you're staying on, Hugo?'

'Herr Schiltz asks me to.'

'Really?'

'He asked you too, didn't he?'

'I had a message via Paula.'

Hugo frowns, and my paranoia begins to fester. What if they're planning something awful? Could Hugo be a part of their plan? All this pretence of showing me the secret room and spying on them. It could all have been a clever ploy to make me feel safe, to mislead me, to lull me into trusting him.

'Ronda?'

'Yes.'

'Where were you? You're not listening. What's wrong?'

'Nothing.'

'Look, Ronda, I may have only known you a couple of days, but I feel as though I know you – if you know what I mean.' He laughs. 'Is there something bothering you? Is it what happened at breakfast?'

'You mean the gun?'

'Well, it's unsettling, isn't it? Dan and Mrs Long were both upset. I had to speak to them.'

'You did?'

'Yes – and Julie, although Mac is there for her.'

I glance at him sideways. He has a strong jaw and dark stubble on his olive coloured, Mediterranean skin.

'How long have you known Herr Schiltz?' I ask.

'Probably about two years.'

'How did you meet him?'

'After a sommeliers' conference. He was staying in the same hotel.'

'In London?'

'No, in France, why?'

'I just wondered.'

'We got chatting, and he liked me. He asked me to his home in Verbier that winter, then to various places in Germany, and also London.'

'Do you work for him most of the time?'

He stretches out his legs. 'I probably could. He certainly pays me enough, but I also work for a few restaurants in the south of France and also in the north of Spain. It's a change of scene, and then when he wants me, I'm available.'

'Do you enjoy it?'

'I like fine wines and—.'

'Women and song?' I quip.

His eyes narrow. 'Champagne mostly.'

I close my eyes and feel the warmth of the sun on my face. After James, I didn't think I'd be interested in anyone for a long time. Now, here I am thinking of Hugo as if he's a potential suitor and I'm on a blind date. My choice in boyfriends, as Tina frequently tells me, is notoriously bad. And, thinking of Hugo, he's educated, handsome, well-travelled and probably an all-round playboy. Even if he were interested, he would just be another lousy option who would inevitably break my heart.

'Can I ask you something, Ronda?' he whispers.

I don't open my eyes, and I murmur, 'Ummm.'

'Would you like to come upstairs with me?'

My eyes fly open, and I suddenly sit up straight and giggle.

'You see, the thing is, I'm not sure what's going on now with the family,' he adds.

'Is it any of your business?'

'Well, actually, yes. I've been the sommelier for most of all Herr Schiltz's business functions for two years, but I don't think that Mike likes me. And, if Herr Schiltz is retiring and no longer working – then I could be out of a job.'

'So you want me to go upstairs with you?' I smile at the irony and my odd perception of our relationship. How can I be so stupid? How could I misread our relationship?

'Well, Ronda, it's a good cover like before, if we get caught. They'll think we're, you know—'

'What?'

'Well, that we're interested in each other – you know, romantically.'

'Ah.'

It was all clear to me now. I had been a convenient ruse for Hugo so that he could go sneaking around the castle listening to conversations while stringing me along and pretending it was all fun and a great adventure. I had been his cover, a fake alibi, in case someone spotted us. That's why he had kissed me, that time when Mrs Long saw us.

I stand up. I've been a complete fool and once again, taken for a ride. It's not Hugo's fault. It's mine. I'm a total numpty with unrealistic expectations. How could a man like Hugo ever be attracted to someone like me? I'm the girl-next-door type.

'Come on then, Hugo. Let's go spying.'

'Really? Thanks, Ronda, you're a real treat.'

'That's what friends are for.'

Chapter 16

*'One-year-olds learn concealment. Five-year-olds lie outright:
they manipulate via flattery. Nine-year-olds – masters of the
cover-up. By the time you enter college, you're going to lie to your
mom in one out of every five interactions.'*
Pamela Meyer

'There's one thing I don't understand,' I say to Hugo as we climb the back staircase. I'm whispering as if the walls have ears. 'Herr Schiltz said that they had camera footage of the person who placed the package on the table. He said that Jim had put hidden cameras around the castle.'

We're walking toward the library. Hugo grins and opens the door and, when he sees it's empty, he pulls me inside.

'That's the funny thing. I saw him do it.' Hugo closes the door behind us, and instinctively I look at the hidden panel behind the books.

'Are we definitely alone?'

Hugo follows my gaze and strides over, releasing the hidden panel lever so the door swings open. The passageway is empty.

'All alone, Ronda. There's no need to worry.'

'I'm paranoid someone will hear us. Where's Jim?'

'He's been sent on an errand to the village.'

Feeling marginally better, I sit on the couch while Hugo walks around the room. He stops to sniff the wine decanter professionally.

'I'll have to organise the wines for tonight.'

'Did you know Jim was spying on everyone?'

'I saw him plant some of the cameras, well, the one in the pantry—'

'Pantry?'

Hugo laughs.

'That's what I thought. It only made sense after you cut the cake and there's the massive rock inside. I suppose no one knew about it, only you and Herr Schiltz, but good old Friedrich wanted to make sure you wouldn't steal it, I suppose. He probably thought you'd run off with it.'

'I hadn't thought of that,' I say truthfully.

'Dear Ronda, you're so lovely and innocent.'

'Tell that to Wilhelm,' I mutter, but he doesn't hear me.

He's looking at the spines of the books on the shelf and reading the titles.

'So, where else did Jim place the cameras – in the Grand Hall obviously, so why didn't he find out who put the package on the table?'

'That's because I found the camera the night before. I saw him place it on the table, near where you put the cake, and it gave him a good view of the whole room, so I thought I'd move it.'

'Didn't he know?'

'Not that I'd done it. I just moved it aside as if it had been knocked accidentally, and so it filmed the wall.'

'Didn't he check it?'

'He did when he woke up, but by that time, I'm guessing

whoever put the package on the table did it late at night or early, first thing in the morning.'

I feel my shoulders slump with relief.

'So, they were bluffing? They have no idea who put the package on the table?'

'Exactly.' Hugo stares into my eyes.

I grin, hardly able to hide my delight.

Hugo frowns. 'But that's the problem, Ronda. I think Herr Schiltz has kept back a few people here, because I think he knows who did it.'

'You mean which one of the guests Gunter, Roma, Mike or Fran put it on the table?'

I have to make sure I'm not a suspect.

'No, no, no, Ronda. It's much more complicated than that. I mean, I think Herr Schiltz knows, at last, he knows who killed his first wife – Iris.'

* * *

There's no sound in the library as I considered Hugo's words. I lean back on the sofa and close my eyes. Is this what Inspector Joachin wanted? Is this why he wanted me to leave the gun on the table?

'You don't think Herr Schiltz could have done it?' I suggest. 'That he might have killed his wife?'

Hugo shakes his head. 'He's not the type. He's a decent man and honourable.'

'I think he's terrifying.'

'Yes, but that's because he reminds you of your father, Ronda. You're confusing the two of them. It's like you've imprinted your father's negative traits onto Herr Schiltz.'

I move toward the door. I'm not ready to be analysed. 'Come on, so what's the plan, Hugo? What are we doing?'

'Well, I thought we'd start upstairs on the battlements with Gunter and Roma. She's fed up that she's not leaving today. She wants to get back to her children.'

'How many do they have?'

'Three. Two boys, ages thirteen and ten and a girl who is five.'

'Who is looking after them?'

'Roma's parents – they live near them in Germany. She's furious because Herr Schiltz changed their plans without asking her. Paula organised it all. Paula must be exhausted. She's coped with all the travel arrangements, castle hire and staff.' Hugo shakes his head. 'I don't know how she's managed it all. They're not particularly kind to her either.'

'You must know Paula quite well?'

'I suppose so.'

'You've worked with her before?'

'Yes, a few times.'

'So, you've grown quite close?' I persist.

'I wouldn't say close. We're always so busy. Did you know about her and Freya?'

'I suspected they were in love. Freya was waiting for phone messages from her, but I think Paula was too frightened in the beginning to text back with all the family around.'

I open the door. 'Where are you going, Ronda?'

'To the battlements, isn't that the idea?'

'Don't you want to know more about Iris Schiltz's death?'

I pause then close the door slowly. 'What do you know? You weren't working for him then.'

'I've looked into it all.'

'Okay, so tell me.'

'Herr Schiltz and Louisa started their affair ten years ago. Iris and everyone else knew, including Fran who was Iris's best friend—'

'She's now Louisa's best friend.'

'She had to be. You see, Mike is Friedrich's business partner. They entertain a lot together, so the ladies have to get on. But, I also think Fran is worried about the business – look at what she said about the import of animals for illegal testing.'

'It's still going on, five years later?'

'I don't know. But presumably, after that lunch, Iris called Gunter, but he was away on business, so she called Wilhelm. He was the last person to see her alive.'

I cover my mouth with my hand. 'It's no wonder Wilhelm was so upset this morning.'

'This morning?'

I tell Hugo how Wilhelm had come to my accommodation and how he had wanted to teach me a lesson.

'He was clearly upset at seeing the gun this morning. It reminded him of his mother's death,' I add.

Hugo listens carefully then he says, 'The police never found the gun – but they accused the gardener, they said he'd been having an affair with Iris. There were witnesses although Fran – her best friend – knew nothing about it.'

'You'd have thought she'd have told her best friend,' I say.

'Well, perhaps not, especially if she's married to the junior partner in the company.'

'That's true. So, who found the body? Who found Iris?'

'Herr Schiltz came home, but she was already dead. Someone had broken in. They smashed the windows. The gardener wouldn't have done that.'

'But they arrested the gardener, and he went to prison, didn't he?'

'Yes, and then he later killed himself,' Hugo adds.

I play along with Hugo. I can't let him know that Inspector Joachin had the gun and he was the one who gave it to me.

'So, now the gun has turned up. Assuming it's the real gun, who has been keeping it all this time? Five years is a long time to hide a murder weapon – it's a very long time, Hugo.'

'Wilhelm was the last person to see her alive.'

'That we know of.'

'True.'

'So why would anyone bring out the gun now?'

Hugo shrugs. 'Maybe, as a warning to his father, if he's thinking of cutting Wilhelm out of the vast majority of the family business by relocating it to Europe.'

'What if it was someone else?' I suggest.

'Like who?'

'It could be anyone. Someone who went to the house after Wilhelm, and shot Iris.'

'Well, it is possible. Wilhelm maintained that he only stayed for a few minutes and that she was alive when he left. Their house is remote. It's in the country and there were no witnesses.'

'But there has to be a motive,' I say. 'Who would want Iris dead? What did she know and who could she have told that made her a threat?'

Hugo shrugs. 'That's what I'd like to know.'

'Well, it points to one person.'

'Who?'

'Herr Schiltz,' I reply, and just at that moment, the door to the library opens.

* * *

Paula pokes her head around the door, and her face shows a sign of relief when she sees it is us.

'Oh, thank goodness, it's you two. I heard voices outside.' She sits down on the sofa. She looks weary and worried. 'It's been madness this morning.'

'You must be exhausted,' Hugo says.

'Well, I'm relieved that at least some of them have gone home. Where's Herr Schiltz?' She looks at Hugo.

'He's gone for a walk to the river with Louisa.'

'Good.' Paula leans her head back and closes her eyes. 'And Jim?'

'He's gone into town on an errand.'

'Even better.'

'Gunter and Roma are on the battlements,' he adds, 'and, Fran and Mike are in their bedroom.'

Paula yawns loudly and covers her mouth.

'So, what's this all about?' I ask her. 'What's going on?'

'I have no idea. Only that Herr Schiltz wants to have time to speak to Gunter and Mike about the business. I suppose, if he's retiring, he wants to make sure the family is organised, and all the finances are in order.'

'What about the gun?' I ask.

Paula opens her eyes. 'That's all a mystery, isn't it? I don't know what to think.'

'Were you working for Herr Schiltz when his first wife died?' I ask.

'I'd only been working with him a few weeks. I was new to the job and it was such a shock.'

'Do you remember what happened?'

'No, not exactly, I was based at the office in Germany in the beginning, and I didn't know what was going on, and then afterwards, after she died, he was off work for a few days. It was all chaotic with the police, interviews, fingerprints, all that sort of thing. We were all questioned. Then they arrested the gardener. His prints were everywhere.'

'Wasn't that because Iris had asked him inside to sort out the house plants?' Hugo says.

Paula shakes her head. 'That's what I heard, but I don't know…' She pauses, 'Weren't you working for him then?'

Hugo shakes his head in denial, and I wonder now how he seems to be well-informed about the events of Iris's death, and how he continually spies on the family.

Hugo said he'd only worked for Herr Schiltz for two years, but he seems very familiar with all the details of the affair, and I begin to wonder how far his loyalty lies. Perhaps he has been working for Herr Schiltz far longer than he admits, or maybe he isn't just a sommelier. He's got the measure of Jim, and it would be typical of a man like Herr Schiltz to employ Hugo as his 'eyes and ears', just like I am, for Inspector Joachin.

Perhaps Hugo is on the family business payroll to watch Herr Schiltz's back. He's extremely loyal to him and never says a bad word.

Was he protecting his boss's bedroom when Jim almost caught me yesterday?

'Do you think Iris was having an affair with the gardener?' he asks.

'Goodness, it was all a long time ago. I only met her once.' Paula checks her clipboard.

'Well,' I say quickly, wanting to make my escape. 'I'll make coffee, and if anyone wants one, I'll be in the kitchen.'

I leave the library, not knowing what to make of Paula or Hugo, or even their relationship and I wonder what Inspector Joachin would make of it all.

***

I take my coffee into the herb garden, and Bobby hops off the wall and flies away as if I've disturbed him. Through the chink in the brickwork, I spy Herr and Frau Schiltz walking across the lawn together. Their stride is purposeful and determined, not like a couple sharing a romantic walk to the river. They're not speaking. I squint in the sunlight, but they are too far away to see if she is still wearing the blue diamond.

Money doesn't make them any happier.

'I thought I'd find you out here.' Mac sits down beside me. 'Are you alright?'

'I'm fine.'

'You seem a little tense today.'

'Just tired.'

'I bought the shopping you requested. It's on the table in the kitchen.'

'Thank you.'

'Is Jim back?'

'I haven't seen him. This is a strange situation, isn't it, Mac? Why do you think this small group are staying on?'

'I have no idea, but they'll be gone tomorrow and then it's back to normal until the next group.'

'When do they arrive?'

'Not until Wednesday. Paula was lucky she could extend their stay for one night.'

'What do you think of Hugo?' I ask.

He pauses before replying, and I'm beginning to get used to the burr of his accent. Whereas Mac is rugged and broad, Hugo is slim and robust, but there's something about them that is similar.

'Hugo is a city boy. He's also very intelligent. I think he's good at what he does – he must be – or Mr Schiltz wouldn't want him around.'

'And Paula?'

'Overworked and underpaid.' He smiles. 'Now, I guess you'll be asking me about Julie next?'

It hadn't been on my list, and I grin at him. 'What do you think of Julie?'

He scratches his head. 'Well, Ma would say not to get involved, she's older than me and—'

I hold up my hand. 'Mac, I asked what *you* think, not what your mother thinks.'

'Julie's lovely. She's adorable, and we get on well.'

'Is there a chance for you romantically?'

He shakes his head. 'I have no idea. She's moved into the village, but she's got a past. She told me that she might not hang around here. She didn't want to tell me too much.'

'Is she separated?'

'Single.'

'What made her come here?'

He seems to think about the answer. 'She's got an aunt in the village.'

'So, she could put down roots?'

'Possibly, possibly – that's what I've been wondering.'

* * *

After I finish my coffee and chatting with Mac, I return to my room to check my phones.

There's no message from Inspector Joachin which annoys me, but back on the bench, sitting in the sunshine, I call Tina.

It clicks to her voicemail, and I wonder what she's doing on Sunday afternoon that she can't take my call. I wish Molly could answer the phone. I miss my morning jog with her. She's uncomplicated and loving. She's all I need.

A shadow descends over me. I squint up into the sunlit sky. Jim stands with his legs akimbo and his arms out wide, like a wrestler's stance, like a man used to his bulky weight.

'I want to talk to you,' he says.

'Hello, Jim, how are you?' I use my friendly tone while calculating how long it would take me to run inside the kitchen and scream for help.

He sits beside me, leaning forward, his elbows on his solid knees.

'I know you went into the Grand Hall early this morning.'

I catch my breath.

He pauses then adds, 'And, I know you were at the table. You could have put the package there.'

I don't say anything, and he looks at me, waiting. 'You're not saying much.'

'You haven't asked me anything, Jim.'

'Did you see anyone else in the room?'

I shake my head. 'Not as far as I can remember.'

'Was anyone else around?'

'Maybe, but if they were, I didn't see them.'

'Freya went into the kitchen.'

'I didn't see Freya. So, that goes to show. You know how big this place is.'

'You went into Herr Schiltz's bedroom yesterday.'

'I was with Hugo on the—'

'So you pretend.'

'Believe what you like.'

'Did you move my camera?'

'What camera?'

He sighs and rubs his eyes with a meaty fist.

'You are the only person I can place this morning, who went to the Grand Hall and was at the dining table.'

'You're missing a massive point.'

'What's that?'

'Where did I get the gun? Well, more than one point actually. There are several points like – how did I get it? How did I know anything about it? Why would I have put it there? How am I involved in this family business?'

He shrugs.

'Exactly, Jim. Your theory doesn't make sense. So, I suggest you stick with the family who employs you and work out why Herr Schiltz has asked only six people to stay behind – including you, Paula and Hugo.'

He stands up and shakes his legs as if his trousers are too tight.

'I saw what you did to Wilhelm, that's not normal – it's professional kickboxing. Where did you learn that?'

'Look, it is normal when you're walking home late at night, in the dark on your own or when someone attacks you on the underground. No one will ever assault me again – ever. And I don't care who they are.'

'Fair enough.'

He turns away and heads toward the kitchen, but he pauses in the doorway and says, 'Don't ever try that fancy stuff with me. I won't be so kind. I'll kill you, cut you into pieces and throw your body in the river.'

Chapter 17

'In any war, there is a concealment of certain kinds of setbacks because it's propaganda for the enemy.'
Kate Adie

The rest of the afternoon is taken up with me preparing canapés and dinner. There hasn't been much time for a rest, and my head is whirling. I'm not only cynical about the events of the weekend, but I'm also angry.

I've done what I had to do. I've planted the package. I've been the eyes and ears for Europol. Now, I may never hear from Inspector Joachin again.

Julie watches me as I roll the pastry for the game pie with frustrated anger. She's working alongside me, but she looks rested, and she's even put on some mascara and lipstick.

'A siesta made all the difference,' she confesses. 'I don't know how you keep going, Ronda.'

'Stubbornness.' I don't smile. 'Pure stubbornness.'

'Are you angry?'

'No, I'm frustrated. I hadn't planned on working tonight. I thought I'd be in the local pub.'

'Do you mind cooking?'

'Sorry, Julie. No, I don't mind. I'm probably overtired.'

'Grumpy more likely.' Hugo breezes into the kitchen.

He looks refreshed, and he's changed into a clean white shirt and navy bowtie.

'I'm here to cheer you both up. Look, see what I've got for us, a lovely bottle of Sancerre to go with our dinner.'

'Pilfering?' I say without looking up.

'No, not at all. Herr Schiltz thought it was a good idea. I did suggest it, I said you'd all worked hard, and as a gesture of goodwill to go with this delicious game pie, it would be appreciated.'

I look up, hiding a smile, wondering how he gets away with it.

Julie looks at the label and appears impressed.

'You're so smooth, Hugo.' She smiles.

'What time are we eating?' Paula comes into the kitchen a few paces behind Hugo.

'The guests are eating at seven. We can sit down at the same time. We can keep an eye on them if they need anything.'

I place the pastry over the first dish and trim the edges. Then repeat the same process for the game pie for the staff.

Hugo winks. 'That looks good enough to eat, Ronda.'

Julie punches him with familiarity on the arm.

Hugo pretends he's injured and rubs his arm. 'They're in the library drinking pre-dinner gin and tonics. Are there any canapés?'

'I'll get them for you,' Julie offers. She returns a few minutes later with trays of salmon blinis. 'Here you go.'

'My goodness, someone has worked hard this afternoon.' Hugo winks at me and then turns his attention to Paula.

'It looks like Louisa has been crying, is she alright?'

'I think so. She says it's hay fever.'

'She's also very quiet,' insists Hugo.

'She's probably just tired.' Paula studies her clipboard.

Jim wanders into the room, and he removes his jacket and rolls up his sleeves. 'What time is dinner?'

'Seven,' Julie answers.

'I'll wait.' Jim pulls out a chair and sits at the table. Then he pulls out his phone, and I know that our conversation now will be guarded, and my mood darkens, I want to be at home.

* * *

I take the starter of fresh crab into the dining hall. My footsteps echo across the old flagstones and the conversation dies, as I feel their eyes on us.

I've insisted on serving them because I want to see them all – I want to find some more clues that I can report back to Inspector Joachin. I don't want him to think I haven't done the best job.

'This looks delicious,' Fran says, as Julie places the starter in front of her. 'I'm quite hungry now.'

Mike remains silent. He tucks his napkin into his navy shirt collar. Gunter looks at his plate appreciatively, but his wife, Roma, doesn't look up.

Although it's her birthday weekend, Louisa looks sullen and her eyes are sad. 'Thank you.'

'I've authorised a bottle of expensive wine for you to share in the kitchen,' Herr Schiltz says.

'So I believe, thank you. We shall enjoy that.' I give a small bow of my head.

'Well, it's not cheap.'

I gaze at Herr Schiltz.

When I was eight, my father bought me a bicycle; a yellow one with a bell and a basket. He used the same tone with me – almost the same words – as Herr Schiltz uses now – *it wasn't cheap* – as if I have to be eternally grateful. My father made me polish the bicycle each time I used it, even though it was barely dirty. I was forced to keep it clean, in good nick, and when I asked why, he looked at me like I was an imbecile.

He replied, 'Because when I sell it, I want to get my money back on it.'

Julie nudges me, and pulls my sleeve, pushing me back toward the kitchen.

'Where were you?' she asks.

I wait until we are safely inside with the door closed before I say, 'He is such an obnoxious little—' I stop.

Jim is staring at me.

Mac frowns.

Paula looks up from her phone.

Hugo spills a drop of wine on the staff dining table and curses quietly.

'Come on,' Julie says. 'Let's start our pie.'

I pull the crusty-topped pie from the oven.

'It looks delicious.' Paula has finally put her clipboard to one side.

The thought of having to serve Herr Schiltz again goes beyond my professionalism. I remember saying to Tina that I wasn't ready for this. I didn't want to come here, and this extra night is pushing me to my limit. But Tina had insisted. We both knew I had to get back to work, and this was supposed to be a good start. It isn't as easy as I'd hoped it would be. I should have known, the minute I met Herr Schiltz in London warning bells had gone off, but I'd ignored them. I was desperate for the money, and the utter humiliation of knowing I'm here because I'm bankrupt and having to keep this secret from everyone is suddenly overwhelming and my eyes well up with tears.

Mac speaks to Jim about the grouse season. Paula checks her notes on her clipboard, and then Hugo and Julie move between the kitchen and dining room with practised ease, as if they've done it hundreds of times before, clearing the starters and serving the main course.

I can't move. I hardly have the motivation to look up.

Julie leaves the dirty dishes on the worktop, and she sits at the table. Suddenly voices in the Grand Hall are raised; an argument?

I look up.

'Where are you from, Paula?' Julie asks. 'You speak fluent German.'

'Originally from America, but my father was in the forces, so we travelled a lot.'

'So, where is your home now?' Julie seems interested.

'Just outside Berlin.'

'Isn't that where they had all the floods in the winter?'

'That was a little further north.'

'Is that near where Herr Schiltz has his home?'

'Um, yes, actually it is.'

'He was lucky not to be affected.' Julie eats slowly.

'His house wasn't affected, but the riverbank burst and some of the buildings were washed away in the local town.'

'I think I read about that,' Julie says. 'Houses, and a supermarket, and a bank.'

Paula eats quickly as if she hasn't eaten in days and speaks with her mouth full. 'There was a problem because a lot of the safety deposit boxes got washed away and some people lost a fortune.'

Julie asks, 'Because they couldn't find everything afterwards?'

Paula says, 'One man had a painting he'd stored in there – it was worth a fortune – and the floodwater ruined it.'

'Was it covered on the insurance?' asks Hugo.

'They didn't want to pay out, anyway, it would cost a lot to be restored, but it would never be the same, you know, with the smell of the river water …it makes an absolute—'

'STOP!' A cry comes from the dining room.

Startled, Paula drops her fork.

'I'VE HAD ENOUGH!' Louisa shouts.

Hugo rushes to the door and looks through the gap.

Jim grabs his jacket from the back of the chair and hurries out of the back door and into the garden.

'FOR GOD'S SAKE, FRIEDRICH! STOP PLAYING GAMES AND TELL US WHAT REALLY HAPPENED TO IRIS!'

Chapter 18

'I believe that mothers should tell the truth, even - no, especially - when the truth is difficult. It's always easier, and in the short term can even feel right, to pretend everything is okay, and to encourage your children to do the same. But concealment leads to shame, and of all hurts shame is the most painful.'
Ayelet Waldman

When Gunter speaks in a quiet voice, Julie leaps to her feet, and Mac leaves the kitchen, following Jim by the back door.

I stand with Paula and Julie, listening to the conversation in the Grand Hall.

Gunter says, 'She's right! You owe it to me, Father. You owe me the truth. Iris is my mother. I am your firstborn.'

Herr Schiltz sits motionless at the head of the table with Louisa on his right and Roma on his left. At the far end of the table, Gunter sits with Mike on his right and Fran, his wife, sits opposite him.

'I owe you nothing. I owe none of you anything.' Herr Schiltz waves his fork in the air, and he continues eating as if Louisa hasn't shouted out.

'Eat!' he demands. 'Eat, all of you. You will need sustenance after I've finished.'

'Did you kill her?' Gunter asks. 'Did you kill my mother?'

Herr Schiltz seems to contemplate his question. 'Is that what you've thought for all these years?'

'IS IT?' Gunter demands.

'Is that what you think of me – your father? That I'm a murderer and I killed my wife.'

'Did you?' Gunter asks.

'No, but I can understand why you might think that.'

'The fact that you discovered her body and there was no murder weapon – wouldn't have made us suspicious?' Gunter's sarcastic tone is bitter.

Beside me, Paula gasps. 'I've never heard him speak to his father like this before.'

'Well, there's a first time for everything,' I reply.

When I turn around, I see now that the men have all disappeared. Julie, Paula and I are the only ones left watching the spectacle through the kitchen door.

'I've told you my version of events many times—'

Gunter interrupts his father. 'Your version of events has gaping holes in it – as you well know – and even the police knew at the time. But without a murder weapon nothing could be proved, could it? But now it's shown up, and quite frankly, Father, your face was a picture. It was as if you'd seen my dead mother all over again – so I will ask you again…' He pauses dramatically. 'Did you kill her?'

'No.'

'Then who had the gun? Why did they leave it here on the table this morning?'

'That's what I have been asking myself. Who had the gun? Who has had it all this time?'

'Well?' prompts Gunter. 'I thought your gorilla had the

whole place wired with cameras to watch and control our every move. Didn't Jim tell you who planted the package under the napkin?'

'The camera had been turned deliberately away, to face the wall.'

'He's useless. He couldn't even get that right!' Gunter reaches for the wine bottle and sloshes the red liquid in his glass. He spills a few drops, and it drips onto the tablecloth, spreading like a bloodstain.

'Do you have to be so vile, Gunter?' Fran asks. 'She wasn't just your mother. She was your father's wife and – my best friend.'

'You've soon changed your allegiance, haven't you?' He laughs sarcastically. 'You were supposed to be her friend. You'd had lunch with her that day, hadn't you? Maybe you followed her back to the house and—'

'Enough!' Mike raises his hand. 'We're not going to sit around here speculating on who might have done it. There is no evidence to suggest that Fran or your father did anything. So, let's get back to the point shall we, Friedrich? Who do you think put the gun under the napkin this morning?'

Friedrich wipes his mouth with his napkin. 'I'm assuming that the person who killed Iris must have kept the gun all these years.'

Fran raises her glass to her lips. 'That's a reasonable conclusion.'

They have all stopped eating. It's another meal ruined, and I despair at the waste.

'So, assuming the murderer kept the weapon – who would that be?'

Mike leans back and surveys the faces at the table before

adding, 'We all flew up here, Friedrich. We couldn't have got it through the airport, unless …'

'Unless what? 'Louisa looks up.

'Unless whoever had it drove up, had it in their possession – in a car.'

Beside me, Paula gasps and covers her mouth with her hand.

'Who drove up?' asks Roma.

Mike stabs the cloth with his index finger. 'Jim and Paula.'

The colour drains from Paula's face. Her eyes are round and frightened. She shakes her head and whispers, 'I didn't.'

Gunter raises his voice. 'I checked with Jim. He told me you wanted him here in case you needed a car urgently, and why would you want that, Father? Why would you need a car?'

'Because of incidents like yesterday when I joined you late for the grouse shooting. I had business to attend to first. I didn't want to hold my family back. It was easier for Jim to drive and us to fly.'

Louisa is staring at her husband.

Fran toys nervously with her napkin.

Mike says, 'It wasn't absolutely necessary though, was it?'

Herr Schiltz tilts his head to look at his business partner.

Gunter stands up.

Mike continues, 'Perhaps you had Jim drive up to Scotland with the revolver, place it on the table to upset us all, then you could accuse whoever you wanted to of killing your wife – when you actually killed her yourself.'

Herr Schiltz shakes his head. 'I loved Iris.'

'You didn't love my mother,' Gunter hisses. 'You've never loved anyone other than yourself. Women are only a convenience for you. Look at Louisa, look at her! She's eye candy for you. She didn't want to stay after Mum died. She wanted to leave you, but she was frightened. And do you know why? Because she thinks you killed Iris too. She's too scared to leave you. She's been scared of you for five years.'

Herr Schiltz turns to look at Louisa.

'Is this true?' he asks softly, but loud enough for us to hear in the kitchen.

She raises her head and looks him in the eye, then very slowly she removes the expensive blue diamond ring he'd placed on her finger only last night.

'Yes. I'm afraid it is.'

* * *

'Paula!' Herr Schiltz sits at the head of the table and shouts, 'Paula, where are you?'

'Oh my goodness,' Paula whispers. She's shaking. 'I'd better go in there.'

Paula straightens her shoulders and walks confidently into the Grand Hall.

'Yes, Herr Schiltz.'

'Please have them clear this mess away. We've lost our appetite. If anyone wants dessert, they can have it later. Tell Ronda to leave it in the kitchen, and everyone can help themselves. In the meantime, we're all going to the library. Tell Hugo to make sure there are drinks available…'

'Yes, sir.' Paula turns to leave.

'And, one more thing.'

Julie and I hold our breath.

Paula waits.

'I don't want us to be disturbed.'

'Very well.'

Paula returns to the kitchen and whispers, 'You heard him?'

'Yes. It's no problem. I'll clear up after they've gone to the library,' Julie says.

'I'll organise dessert,' I add.

My hands are shaking. The mention of the gun and the mystery of who put it there is still a secret – my secret. I'm curious to see how this is playing out and how Mike has come to the logical conclusion that they'd never have got the gun through airport security.

I'm fortunate that Hugo moved the camera. I've been lucky, and I'm overcome with a sense of euphoria only interrupted by the thought that Herr Schiltz now seems to be implicated in Iris's murder.

Could this be true?

Did Inspector Joachin suspect this?

Perhaps Herr Schiltz did hide the gun in the bank. If he put it in the bank safety deposit box and it got washed away during the heavy storms in Germany, then it would make sense. The police found it, and that's how it came into the possession of Inspector Joachin.

Which would mean that Herr Schiltz probably did kill his first wife.

* * *

After the guests are nestled in the library, the dining table is clear, and I've organised dessert. Julie is stacking the dishwasher.

'I've got tummy cramps, Julie. Is it okay for me to leave you to tidy up?'

'No problem,' she replies.

I can tell she's not happy. She also thinks I'm lying.

I wait until she goes into the Grand Hall for a last tidy up and I'm alone in the kitchen and then I run up the backstairs. I find the secret panel, the secret door clicks open, and I step inside; moving quietly and slowly I find my way, using my phone torch. A hand comes out of the darkness and grips my wrist. Another covers my mouth.

Instinctively I twist away.

'Shush,' Hugo whispers angrily in my ear. 'Turn off the torch.'

'Move over.' I push him, but he's solid muscle.

Then he shifts his position to let me peer through the slats as we did before, crouched uncomfortably, shoulder to shoulder, breathing in each other's stale air.

In the library, Herr Schiltz's voice is measured and calm. He stands in front of the others like a teacher.

'I'm going to tell you the events of the night my wife died. I'll ask you all to trust me. I have never lied to you before. I have always looked after my family, but on this occasion, I think you'll agree with my actions.'

Louisa and Fran sit together on the sofa. At right angles, on two single chairs, Gunter sits with Roma. Only Mike sits alone in a chair with his legs crossed nursing a brandy.

'On the day of Iris's death, she and Fran went shopping. They had a late lunch and Iris returned home just after four o'clock. I don't know what she did for those few hours until I arrived at our home a little after seven, but when I opened the front door, she was lying on the floor in the living room – dead.'

Fran shakes her head.

Louisa stares at her husband.

He adds, 'There was a note—'

'A note?' Louisa cries. 'A note?'

'Yes. I didn't see it at first. All I could see was Wilhelm crying.'

'Wilhelm was there?' Gunter says. 'He was in the house?'

Herr Schiltz holds up his hand and waits for silence before he continues.

'He had arrived minutes before me, but I didn't know that at the time. I saw him crying. He was distressed. Jim had dropped me at home, and he hadn't gone far, so I called him back. I put Wilhelm in my car and told Jim to drive him home. I also gave Jim the murder weapon. I gave him the gun, and I told him to take it to the bank first thing in the morning and put it in the safety deposit box.'

'You tampered with the evidence?' Fran says.

'Hear me out, please. It was all over in a matter of minutes. No reasonable time delay, and I called the police immediately. I thought that with Wilhelm out of the way I could cover for him. Then I called you, Gunter, if you remember, I told you that Iris was dead and I told you I had also called Wilhelm, but what I didn't tell you was that Jim answered Wilhelm's phone – to give him an alibi. I stayed on the phone for an appropriate amount of time. That, I thought, would ensure that the police would see how distressed you both were. I knew the police would think it was me who killed Iris, but without a murder weapon – they couldn't prove it.'

'You bribed the police though, didn't you?' Gunter says.

Herr Schiltz ignores his son. 'Iris died an hour before I got home. The only problem I had was that Wilhelm's car was still at the house. I didn't know how to get rid of it, and then I saw the gardener.'

'You framed him?' Fran sounds incredulous.

'I asked him to take Wilhelm's car to his house. I gave him the cash I found in Iris's handbag.'

'So that when the police found him, you pretended he had killed Iris, stolen money and taken the car.' Roma shakes her head in disbelief. 'They believed you and not him. He was an innocent man.'

'I know. I'm sorry. You will never know how sorry.'

'We need to call the police.' Roma looks at Gunter for support.

'Wait.' Herr Schiltz sips his brandy. 'I haven't finished. There's more. Let me tell you what happened. I'd seen Wilhelm distressed and leaning over his mother's body and I'd assumed he'd killed her. I'd taken the gun because I wanted to protect him. I realised very quickly that I'd lost Iris, but I wasn't about to lose my son as well. I wasn't going to let him go to prison.'

'But Iris had been killed,' Roma cries. 'She was dead. Can't you see anything wrong with that?'

'I love my son,' Herr Schiltz shouts back.

'That's not the point. An innocent man killed himself in prison because you lied to protect your son.'

'I lied to protect my family. Imagine if the press had got hold of the fact Wilhelm killed his mother.'

'But why would Wilhelm do that?' Fran asks. 'If Wilhelm was guilty—'

'He was angry with her,' Gunter replies. He speaks matter-of-factly as if he'd been through everything in his head countless times. 'He was angry with her because she didn't stand up for herself. We all knew that our father was having an affair. We were ridiculed and taunted at school, and our mother was a laughing stock amongst friends. You, Fran, were the only person she trusted – and the only friend to show kindness.'

'You knew about your father and Louisa's affair?' Fran asks.

'I knew for years, but when Wilhelm found out, it was hard for him to understand. When he—' he points to his father '—stayed away for nights and went on a separate summer holiday each year, Wilhelm couldn't cope. He began to hate her. He blamed our mother for his misery – and the fact our father strayed from our family home.'

'Why didn't he blame your father?' Fran asks.

'Because he knew he would have to work with him one day. After he left school, Wilhelm knew that he would have to swallow his pride. So, he turned his anger on our mother. He believed she didn't try hard enough to please our father, both in and out of bed, and I couldn't reason with him.'

'But you tried?' asks Roma.

'Of course.'

'Wilhelm loved her.' Fran shakes her head. 'He loved her. How could he …?'

'He didn't murder her,' Herr Schiltz says quietly.

'What?'

Louisa looks up.

Gunter frowns.

Roma places her drink on the table.

Herr Schiltz looks exhausted. 'The story gets worse, bear with me…'

* * *

I don't realise that I'm leaning against Hugo until he moves and I realign my position in the cramped space. It's hot, and Hugo's presence beside me is both reassuring and disturbing.

I am Inspector Joachin's eyes and ears, but will he believe

me?

This is a confession – Herr Schiltz's confession – how will I be able to prove any of this?

If only I had a camcorder or something to tape this conversation. I glance down at my phone, wondering if the sound would be too muffled.

'You'd better get on with it, Friedrich,' Mike says. 'All of us are finding this very distressing, especially Louisa.'

Herr Schiltz stands taller and appears to be in no hurry to put them out of their misery.

'After looking after Wilhelm, the following day Jim took the gun to my safety deposit box in the bank. Then, last winter, it got swept away, in the storms.'

'It was never found?' asks Mike. He leans forward and places his cup on the table.

'No, and until then, it was in my possession all the time, in the bank.'

'Did you get it dusted for fingerprints?' he insists.

'No.'

Mike shakes his head. 'Well, they probably won't show up on the gun now. There's still no proof that Wilhelm might or might not have done it.' Mike sighs and sips his brandy.

'Well, that's the thing, Mike. I know that he didn't do it. He definitely didn't because someone else visited Iris after she came back from her lunch and shopping trip with Fran before Wilhelm arrived.'

'Who?' asks Louisa.

'Well, let me ask Fran.'

'Me?' Fran looks shocked. 'I didn't see her again.'

'I'd like to know what you discussed with her at lunch.'

Fran looks at the five faces focused on her. 'I can't remember.

It was a long time ago …'

'Yes, you can. It was crucial, Fran. It was urgent. So much so that she tried to phone me. But I was in an important meeting, and I didn't want to be disturbed. I had three missed calls from her. When she didn't pick up her phone, I drove straight home. In her message, she told me it was urgent. She needed to speak to me.'

Fran shakes her head. 'I can't remember.'

'Yes, you can. Be brave.' Herr Schiltz lifts the bottle of reserve brandy in his hands. 'Anyone for a top-up?'

No one replies, so he refills his glass.

I wish I could have one. My throat is dry, and I feel as though I'm going to pass out with the heat.

'Well? Have you remembered, Fran? Or would you like me to tell everyone?'

Fran crosses her legs and looks uncomfortable.

Herr Schiltz continues, 'You'd found out some details about our company, a recent business deal, that affected you.'

'No, no, I know nothing about—'

'Let me finish. I believe you told Iris that we, our company that usually imports and exports valuable artefacts for museums and galleries, was a ruse and that we were really importing valuable animals used for illegal testing to make drugs.'

Fran stares at him.

'Is this true?' Louisa asks. She has more colour in her cheeks, and she leans forward holding out her glass. 'I'd like a top-up, Friedrich, please.'

'Of course it's true, Louisa. I have nothing to gain by lying to any of you here tonight. Fran met Iris for lunch, and by the time they were finished, Iris was furious. And, as Gunter says, it was bad enough that I was having an affair but then finding out I was behaving illegally and involving her sons in this business was the end for her. She wanted to protect Gunter and Wilhelm like any mother would. Now, Gunter was away and I was in a meeting, so the next person she called—'

'Was Wilhelm?' Louisa interrupts.

'No, it was Mike.'

'Mike,' Fran gasps.

'What?'

Louisa grabs the bottle from Friedrich's hand and slops a decent measure into her glass.

Gunter looks at Mike.

'Is this true?'

Mike shakes his head. 'No.'

'It's alright, Mike. I can prove it.'

'Then why didn't you say anything before?' complains Gunter.

'Because it isn't true.' Mike stands up. 'You're making up lies because you're about to resign.' Mike stares stonily at his business partner.

'That's precisely why I'm bringing it up this weekend. I was intent on resigning after I found out what you've been doing behind my back for the past five years, but then the gun mysteriously appeared and it brought up old memories. Now, I have no option but to put this to rest once and for all.'

Mike stands up and faces his business partner. 'You have no proof of any of this, and it's beginning to sound like sour grapes, Friedrich. This business would have gone bust a long time ago if it wasn't for me.'

'I turned a blind eye, Mike, because I thought you were a loyal friend. But when Louisa told me how Fran had spoken to her urgently yesterday – about the same concerns – I now realise that's not true. Not only have you let me down as a business partner, but you also killed my wife.'

Chapter 19

'Choose silence of all virtues, for by it you hear other men's imperfections, and conceal your own.'
George Bernard Shaw

'Before you continue with these wild accusations, Friedrich, I suggest you provide the proof because that's what the police will be looking for,' Mike replies.

Herr Schiltz replies calmly, 'They barely questioned you the last time, did they, Mike? But Iris did phone you. You said to the police she'd called you looking for me, but that's not true, is it? She called you because she wanted to speak to *you*.'

Mike stands his ground defiantly, and in my ear, Hugo breathes quietly and regularly. My legs are developing cramp, and I wonder if Hugo feels the same.

'After you spoke to her, you went to my house.' Herr Schiltz touches his moustache.

'Not true.'

'Iris told you she knew what you were doing. She knew it was illegal and she told you she would tell me.'

'Not true.'

'You argued.'

'No.'

'You killed her.'

'Is that as far as you can go with your wild accusations?'

'They're not wild. I know for a fact. You see, Wilhelm told me.'

'Told you what?'

'The thing is, Mike, none of it made any sense. I knew Wilhelm loved his mother, and when I got home, he was covered in her blood – I assumed the worst. I acted too quickly, but he couldn't speak. I saw him kneeling at her side, and the gun was on the floor and all the blood. It was a shock. I had to get him out of there and, you know, he had treatment for many years after that. It was our secret. He thought he'd killed her and I'd covered for him. He still has PTSD, but he told me this weekend, last night, that he remembered. He said she was dead when he arrived home – but he knew you'd been in the house.'

'How could he have known?'

'That's what happens with PTSD. It's often a trigger that can set all the memories off again. That's why he went a bit crazy this weekend. He couldn't work it out. And I didn't want him to stay here. I wanted him as far away as possible until I can finally sort this out, once and for all.'

'What was the trigger?' asks Louisa. 'The PTSD?'

Herr Schiltz smiles. It isn't a kind smile.

'He remembered your aftershave, Mike. Do you remember on Friday, in here, in the library he was obsessed about a smell? He seemed confused, but it was gnawing away in his memory. And when you came down to breakfast yesterday, he found it overpowering and because all the family were together, all the memories came flooding back to him, and he remembered. He told me this morning, again.'

'That's impossible,' Mike says.

'You're the only person I know who wears that particular brand of aftershave, and you've hardly seen him since Iris died because a few weeks after the funeral, I sent Wilhelm to America where I hoped he would get strong and be able to start again. That's why he went off the rails this weekend. It was the smell. It was a mind association. He knew someone had been there in the house with Iris, and he had that recollection, but because the gardener was the accused, Wilhelm went along with it all.'

'That's ridiculous.' Mike shakes his head in defiance.

'This weekend is the first time you've been in his company for years. He recognised your scent – your aftershave.'

'Impossible and far-fetched,' Mike says dismissively. 'Now, I've heard enough of your wild tales. I think this weekend has been a strain – a very emotional one for you – especially now that you've announced your resignation.'

'I announced my resignation because I'm winding down the imports and exports from China before I go. Paula has been in contact with the lawyers carrying instructions to the managers in all departments with that news.'

'She can't do that—'

'I know you've slipped some illegal goods through in the last few years, and I wasn't quick enough to stop you, but by closing down America, the illegal side of the business – will stop.'

'That's ridiculous. You can't do that.'

Herr Schiltz stands his ground.

'Fran, tell us all the truth now. When you had lunch with Iris on the day she died, did you tell her about Mike's illegal dealings?'

Fran looks wide-eyed and frightened, but then she nods her head. 'Yes. I did.'

'And what did Iris say?'

'She was furious. She said she was going to talk to you. I told the police.'

'I know you did, and she did try and speak to me, but then Mike was in my office that afternoon when she called to speak to me. I suspect she argued with you, and you were frightened she'd tell me, so you left the office and you went to our home.'

Mike looks at Herr Schiltz in disbelief.

'You took a gun, Mike. And when you got there, she told you she was going to tell me.'

'No.' Mike's protest is weaker, his voice smaller.

'You fired the gun. You killed Iris.'

Mike shakes his head.

'Why didn't you ever check the gun for fingerprints?' asks Roma.

'I didn't know until this weekend until Wilhelm came to me this morning. Before that, I never wanted to bring it all up. I wanted it all to be forgotten.'

'It could have stayed in the bank forever,' says Fran.

'And Mike would have been protected,' adds Louisa, toying with her brandy glass. 'But then the rain came, and the riverbank and foundations of the bank were swept away,' she adds.

'Yes.'

'So, who found the gun?' Gunter asks. 'And brought it here this weekend?'

Herr Schiltz frowns. 'I don't know.'

'The police?' asks Roma.

'How would the police know that it came from Friedrich's

safety deposit box?' she asks.

Herr Schiltz looks thoughtful, and I hold my breath, knowing I'm the only one who knows the answer to that question.

'It wouldn't have taken the police long to associate the missing gun with the one that killed Iris and the coincidence of you having valuables locked away in the same bank.' Louisa stands up. 'Maybe they think you did it, Friedrich?'

'Do you think the police are here?' Roma asks.

Herr Schiltz frowns.

Louisa is gaining confidence. 'Maybe that's why they put it on the breakfast table, in the hope the family would turn on each other and find out the truth.'

'And you have,' says Roma. 'Mike, it will probably be easier for you if you confess.'

Mike swallows the last of his brandy. 'Never.'

Fran sits forward and clutches her hands together. 'It was you, Mike. I blocked it all out. I was so upset about Iris, and I didn't want to be responsible for her death, but it's true. After I found out about the illegal imports, you threatened me, and I'd never seen you so angry, you even—'

'Shut up, Fran!'

'I was scared,' she adds.

'Don't be stupid, woman. Now, let's forget this silly nonsense. I want some dessert. What about you, Louisa? Roma?'

No one moves.

Herr Schiltz stands in his way, blocking his path from the library. 'I'll prove it, Mike. I promise you. Because Iris had left a note and it made no sense at the time, but it does now.'

'You've still got the note?' Gunter cries.

'I've kept it in my wallet ever since.'

'You didn't show it to the police?' says Roma.

'I thought it might incriminate Wilhelm.'

'What does the note say?' Gunter asks.

Herr Schiltz pulls it from his wallet, and that's when I sneeze.

* * *

It comes from nowhere. It takes me by surprise, and it comes out in a sudden rush. *Whoosh.*

Hugo is like a hare on a racing track. He moves quickly, pushing me ahead of him, through the back passageway and into the light of the corridor onto the back staircase.

Behind us, there are heavy footsteps. Someone curses in the darkness. Hugo slams the secret panel door and pulls me down the stone steps to the kitchen. We pause breathlessly for a second, but then he takes my hand and leads me quickly outside to the bench in the herb garden where we sit and catch our breath.

My hands are in my lap.

He's looking over my shoulder at the doorway then suddenly he leans forward and kisses me. It takes me by surprise. His lips are soft and warm, and his tongue gently probes my mouth. I recover quickly because my arms are suddenly around his neck, and I've opened myself up to him.

'Hey!'

I pull away.

Jim is in the doorway looking flustered as if he's run down a flight of stairs and through the kitchen. He looks as if he's searching for something – someone.

'What?' Hugo jumps to his feet, appearing guilty at having been caught kissing me. I bow my head and look worried, no great acting job because my heart is thumping with fear and also excitement. James had never kissed me like that.

'Who was upstairs just now?' Jim calls.

Hugo shrugs. 'I don't know. Do they want something?' Hugo moves to walk past Jim and go inside, as if he's on duty, but Jim places a hand on his chest.

'You're breathing hard,' he says.

'Wouldn't you be?' Hugo nods at me.

'Where were you just now?'

Hugo opens his arms. 'Well, it's not rocket science is it? But please don't tell Herr Schiltz. He might disapprove, and I don't want him to think—'

'Shut up. He's got other things on his mind. Where's Paula? Where's Julie and that guy from the estate, Mac?'

'They were here. We've all been here, but the family were busy. They didn't want to be disturbed. If there's anything they need…' He turns to me. 'Ronda, come into the kitchen with me.'

I stand up obediently, and Jim regards me warily.

'Did you sneeze?' he asks.

I frown at Jim as if he has lost the plot. 'I think Hugo would have noticed if I did.'

Hugo bursts into laughter.

Jim disappears in the direction of the Grand Hall and while I'm smiling Hugo places a finger to his lips in a warning and says loudly, 'Perhaps we should go upstairs and see if our guests would like anything?'

I follow Hugo up the stairs to the library, still feeling his burning kiss on my lips.

* * *

Hugo taps on the library door, and we both wait.

It's Herr Schiltz who responds.

'Come in.'

Hugo opens the door cautiously, and with enough leverage so I can see the guests inside. They seem to be in disarray.

Fran is crying, and Louisa is sitting with her arm around her shoulders. Roma is on her phone, and only Herr Schiltz looks confused.

'Jim came into the kitchen. We just wanted to check to see if you need anything?'

'Where is Jim?' Herr Schiltz asks.

'He was in the garden – looking for someone. He mentioned about someone sneezing?'

Herr Schiltz asks, 'Where were you?'

'Downstairs, sir. Waiting in the herb garden in case you need—'

'Were you behind that bloody panel?' He points at the bookcase.

Hugo shakes his head solemnly. 'No, sir.'

Herr Schiltz shouts, 'Where's Paula? Where is everyone?'

I glance into the corridor and to the stairs that lead to the small hall and the battlements.

Herr Schiltz pushes past us.

Louisa calls, 'Hugo, please look after Friedrich. He's looking for Gunter and Mike – there's been a problem.'

'What can I do?' Hugo asks.

'Follow him. Make sure no one gets hurt. Roma, have you called the police yet?'

'Very well,' Hugo says. He whispers to me. 'Go downstairs, Ronda. Stay in the kitchen. Stay out of the way until the police arrive.'

'What about you?'

'I'll find Herr Schiltz and bring him back here.'

'What about Gunter and Mike?'

'Stay in the kitchen, Ronda. Go on!' Hugo pushes me toward the stairs, and then he turns in the opposite direction and taking the steps two at a time, he heads up to the next floor and the ramparts of the battlements.

When I glance into the library, the three ladies are huddled on the sofa together. Roma is speaking quietly into her phone, and I guess she's got through to the local police.

'I know he did it,' Fran sobs. 'I just know in my heart. Everything Friedrich said was true. I lied to the police. I told them Mike had come home earlier than he did, and I shouldn't have done. Oh, Louisa, what have I done?'

'Don't cry; come on.' Louisa strokes her friend's hair. 'You couldn't help it. Mike has bullied you for years.'

'But what sort of a friend am I? I didn't even help Iris.'

'Shush, Fran …' Louisa is staring at the floor. 'Don't cry. It's too late now. It's far too late for tears.'

Chapter 20

'When someone has spent a lifetime trying to survive a death sentence, the last thing you want is your children uncovering what you have been at such pains to conceal.'
Michael Korda

Instead of heading to the kitchen as Hugo told me, I run up the stone steps; the door of the small hall is open, and I glance inside. It's empty, so I venture up the next flight of steps to the battlements.

The door is ajar, and I hear voices. I peer cautiously through the gap and standing in front of me, Gunter and Mike are speaking quietly. There's no sign of Hugo.

'That didn't go well, did it?' Mike says, calmly lighting a cigar.

'No,' agrees Gunter. 'You need to get the gun. It's the only thing they can link back to you.'

They're leaning companionably on the wall, gazing out at the river and trees beyond, Mike sighs.

'Yes. I need to get the gun back from Friedrich. Stupid old man. I'll go into his room later.'

'What about Louisa and Fran?'

'I can sort Fran out. She's my wife. She'll do as she's told.

What about Roma, can you handle her?'

'She doesn't know I'm involved, so I want to keep it that way.'

'You'd sacrifice me to keep your name out of it all?'

'I wasn't the one who killed Iris. You said it was the only option. I trusted you, Mike. But she was still my mother.'

'That bloody Wilhelm, how could he recognise my aftershave?'

Gunter turns to face him, and I dodge back so he can't see me in his peripheral vision.

'He's a smart boy. That's why I was pleased when my father sent him away. It's the best thing he did, get him out of our way. But he's unhinged. You could see that this weekend. He was looking for a fight.'

'It's always amazed me that there's no love lost between you two.' Mike sucks on his cigar.

'He's spoilt. You can see the way Papa defended him. He wouldn't have done that for me.'

There are footsteps on the stairs behind me, and I freeze. I can't go onto the roof. There's no way down, but there is a small cupboard. I pull open the door and step over a bucket and mop before pulling the door closed.

Footsteps rush past. I wait, holding my breath and when I think it's clear, I push open the door and step quietly into the corridor. The entrance to the battlements swings open, and I check to make sure there's no one behind me.

Gunter and Mike are facing Herr Schiltz and Jim.

'Gunter?' shouts Herr Schiltz. 'Tell me you're not involved in any of this.'

'I'm not.'

'Then stand away from Mike. We've called the police.'

Gunter doesn't move. 'That's a bit drastic, Papa. Mike's your business partner.'

'Not anymore.'

'You're basing your accusations on Wilhelm's ability to smell and recognise Mike's aftershave.' Gunter laughs. 'That won't stand up in court.'

'We also have Fran's testimony.'

'Fran won't testify.' Mike leans confidently against the wall. 'You're making a fool of yourself, Friedrich.'

'I have a gun.'

'There won't be any evidence on that, not after five years locked away and then washed in a dirty river.'

'They'll trace it back to who bought it.' Herr Schiltz's voice doesn't sound so confident now, and beside him Jim stands like a wrestler waiting to get in the ring.

'That's impossible.' Mike laughs. 'You should give up and join us. There's no need to resign and close down some of the company. Take some time off, go to the Caribbean with Louisa, enjoy your retirement.'

'You killed my wife.'

'You didn't love her.'

'I did. I did love her once – it just changed, that's all.' He raises his voice. 'She was your mother, Gunter. Mike killed your mother – how does that make you feel?'

'She loved Wilhelm more.'

'You were always a jealous boy, but we can sort this out. Come down to the library, Gunter. We can wait for the police in there.'

'I'm happy out here with Mike.'

'And I can finish this.' Mike waves his cigar in the air.

'I don't want to ask Jim to take you down.'

'Then don't.'

It's a standoff but then Herr Schiltz moves forward, and he reaches out for his son. 'I'm surprised at you, Gunter, you knew all along?'

'I guessed,' he lies.

'But you didn't do anything? You didn't tell me?'

'You were busy protecting Wilhelm. What did you want me to do?'

'You're involved in the illegal shipments from China, aren't you?' Herr Schiltz steps back as if realising for the first time that his eldest son is involved.

Gunter laughs. 'What do you want? A taped confession?'

'This is between us as a family.' Herr Schiltz reaches out, but Gunter bats his father's hand away and Herr Schiltz loses his balance.

Quickly, Jim steps forward and grabs Gunter's wrist. He twists him roughly, pulling his arm behind his back and he shoves him against the wall.

Gunter tries to pull away, and a scuffle takes place, but Herr Schiltz is knocked over and he falls to the floor.

Jim wraps Gunter in a stranglehold then it all happens quickly. Mike is running at full speed toward me, hurling himself through the door where I'm standing. He pushes me aside, and I fall back against the wall, watching him leap down the stairs.

I leave the men wrestling on the battlements and run after Mike, down the stairs and past the library.

Roma calls out, 'Gunter, is that you?

Louisa is on her feet, and I slow my pace.

'Ronda? Where's Friedrich?'

'On the battlements.' I don't stop. I'm running again, down

the stairs, jumping the last few steps through the empty kitchen and out into the herb garden. I run past the bench, along the path, then I see Mike running across the gravel to Mac's parked Land Rover.

I chase him at full speed and just as he opens the car door, I reach it first, and I slam it shut.

'Ronda?' he cries. 'Get the fu—get off!'

'I'm not letting you go.'

He raises his fist and hits me on the cheek. He catches me by surprise, knocking me off my feet. I fall onto the gravel, and it scrapes my palms.

I jump up. Mike has one foot inside the car. He's off-balance so I grab the back of his shirt collar and pull him roughly away, and then I take up my kickboxing stance.

He hurls himself at me. I lift my knee, and I snap it to the left, striking him on the inside of his thigh in a side knee kick. I spin and side-elbow him in the cheekbone, then turning quickly I use my left arm to strike his nose. I hear it break as I downward elbow and hit him on the forehead.

'Freeze!' a voice shouts.

I move quickly and raise my left knee to my chest, flex my foot and lead with my heel and kick him with all my force in the chest.

Mike collapses, winded, on the ground.

'Police! Don't move!'

From the corner of my eye, Julie moves forward holding a gun. Behind her, Mac is holding a rifle, and Hugo is smiling at me.

'Great drop kick, Ronda!' he laughs.

Chapter 21

'To conceal anything from those to whom I am attached, is not in my nature. I can never close my lips where I have opened my heart.'
Charles Dickens

I sit on the grass verge in front of Castle Calder's magnificent entrance. Julie is dressed in jeans and a cream blouse, as she was earlier, but without the apron. I watch her handcuff Mike to the steering wheel of the Land Rover. He's groaning and clutching his bleeding nose, but Julie ignores him. Meanwhile, I'm trying to piece everything together.

Hugo says, 'Great job, Ronda. Mac, come with me. Let's check on things inside.'

The two men disappear without a backward glance, and I wait for Julie to join me.

'You're police?' I ask.

'Yes, I'm with Police Scotland, here in Aberdeen.'

'Did you put the package in my bedroom?'

'Yes.'

'And, you know Inspector Joachin?'

'Inspector Joachin García Abascal?'

'Yes, that's the one.'

She thinks for a minute. 'I met him briefly. He's with the International Crime Squad at Europol. They have no jurisdiction in Scotland. They asked for our help.'

'Help?'

'Yes, they were tracking down a valuable stolen diamond.'

'Diamond?' I can't hide my surprise.

'It's rare and valuable, presumably worth a couple of million. You know, the blue diamond? Mr Schiltz bought it on the black market a few months ago – back in January.' She smiles.

'I thought this was all about the murder of his first wife.'

She smiles. 'After Herr Schiltz bought the diamond on the black market, from a Russian dealer, the inspector did his homework. He found out that Herr Schiltz kept the diamond in a safety deposit box in a bank in Germany. It so happened, it was one of the items that got swept away in the storm, but they found it. Unfortunately, Herr Schiltz was greedy. He tried to claim on the insurance but they were suspicious of him.'

I shake my head, taking in all the information.

Julie continues, 'and, when the German police found the gun, the inspector wanted to nail Herr Schiltz for the murder of his wife too. We all thought that he had killed his wife – that's why he hid the gun – until this weekend.'

I sit up, hugging my knees.

'You need some ice on that cheek of yours, Ronda. You'll have a nasty bruise on your face.'

I ignore Julie, concentrating, trying to make sense of what's happened over the weekend.

She sees my confusion because she grins and says, 'We knew that they had a reservation here at Castle Calder for the weekend. So, I came on ahead, though I wasn't sure Mrs

Long would give me the job.'

'You're good in the kitchen.'

'Thank you, but I only got through it thanks to you.'

'You're undercover?'

'Yes.'

'You're a good policewoman too.' I punch her arm. 'I'd never have guessed.'

'That's the idea, Ronda.'

'But I took all the risks.' I shake my head. 'I put the gun in the napkin.'

'We were watching you, all the time.'

'So, Inspector Joachin asked me to put the gun on the table to confront Herr Schiltz, but he was really after the ring, the ring he'd given his wife the night before?'

Julie nods.

'You texted him the first evening to say you'd put the ring in the cake. So, we knew where it was all the time. That was the easy part. Afterwards, it was just a case of stirring up the family to clear up a five-year-old murder case—'

'In Germany.'

'Exactly.'

'And, you do this for a living?'

'Yes.' Julie smiles and I can see now that she's an attractive girl.

'What about Mac? Did he know?'

'Only a few hours ago. I managed to get him and Paula out of the way. I had to keep them safe. I couldn't take a chance it wouldn't turn nasty. One of them may have had another weapon. But it was great to have Mac to back me up, especially with Jim around.'

'And what about Hugo?' I ask.

Julie jumps to her feet as a black Mercedes comes through the front gate and up the gravel drive.

'He's a great sommelier,' she replies. She adds with a grin, 'And here comes our big boss.'

* * *

Inspector Joachin García Abascal climbs out of the car. He's dressed casually in beige chinos and an olive-green linen jacket. With him is a tall slim lady in a sharp navy suit and white blouse.

'Hello, Ronda. I'm Inspector Niven.' She smiles but her face is narrow and her eyes sharp.

Inspector Joachin holds out his arms. 'Sorry I'm late. I had to make a few phone calls. Ronda – thank you!' He takes me by the shoulders and kisses me – Spanish-style – on both cheeks. 'Oh, that's a nasty bruise, who did that?'

'Him.'

I nod at Mike, handcuffed to the car steering wheel. 'But he's stopped whingeing now.'

'Well, I believe you got him back with a very smooth drop kick.'

I blink surprised. 'You know everything?

'Almost.' Inspector Joachin grins.

I can't help but think what a lovely kind smile he has and I glance down to check the wedding band on his finger.

'And, Julie. Congratulations!' He turns, and he kisses her too, in his smooth European fashion. 'Thank you. Your work has been exemplary. I believe Chief Inspector McGrath will be thanking you in person at a later date.'

Julie beams. I can tell she's as charmed by Inspector Joachin as I am.

He turns away and walks towards the Land Rover.

'Well done, Julie.' Inspector Niven smiles. 'We'll chat later.'

Julie nods.

'Hello, Michael,' Inspector Joachin announces, 'The police will take you to the police station shortly, and charge you for the trade of illegal animals from China into America. The German police want to interview you for the murder of Iris Schiltz, five years ago. They are also investigating the company where you are managing director. And I don't take it lightly that you assaulted Ronda. No real man hits a woman but then again, I think, to your eternal embarrassment, you found that out yourself. It will be up to her if she presses charges – however, I do believe that will be the least of your concerns.'

A police car with a flashing light comes quickly up the driveway, followed by two black vans.

'Ah, good. Reinforcements.' Joachin smiles. He turns to me and asks, 'Now, where are the rest of the family, Ronda?'

'I believe they're in the library.'

'Would you like to show me the way? Julie, we'll leave you here to liaise with these police officers.'

He nods at the men already climbing out of the van, and Inspector Niven follows us, appearing quite happy to leave everything to Inspector Joachin.

* * *

I lead Inspector Joachin and Inspector Niven inside Castle Calder. We walk around the garden and through the kitchen, but he pauses in the corridor.

'Is that the pantry,' he asks, 'where the cake was kept?'

'Yes.' I smile.

He grins back. 'Excellent work.'

Upstairs the library door is open, and Hugo is standing inside waiting for us.

Louisa and Fran are still sitting on the sofa. Roma is by the window looking down at the events playing out on the drive with Mike and the police officers as he's led away to the police van.

Jim is standing behind Gunter who sits morosely in a hard-backed chair. And Herr Schiltz looks dazed, sad and contemplative.

'Good evening, everyone. My name is Inspector Joachin García Abascal from Europol, and this is my colleague, Inspector Niven, from Police Scotland.'

'Good evening.' Inspector Niven moves forward and stands in front of Louisa.

'Please may I see that ring?' She points at the blue diamond.

In all the excitement of events, I hadn't noticed the diamond ring back on Louisa Schiltz's finger. I know she'd taken it off but somehow and at some time, Herr Schiltz must have persuaded her to wear it again.

Herr Schiltz groans as Louisa pulls the diamond ring from her finger.

'Here!' she says, thrusting it at Inspector Niven but it's Inspector Joachin who steps forward with his hand outstretched. She drops it in his palm as if she's pleased to be rid of it.

'Thank you.' He lifts it to the light and smiles. 'This is what we wanted, thank you.'

'The ring?' exclaims Fran. 'You wanted that bloody ring? What about Iris?'

'Ah, yes. Well, we were after the ring, but it was also good to get a confession or almost a confession to Iris's murder.'

Gunter speaks slowly. 'You wanted the ring?'

'Yes, but with a little more work, I'm fully confident that the German police will have all the evidence they need. I think the truth about what happened five years ago to your mother has finally come to light.' Inspector Joachin meets Gunter's hard stare.

Gunter says dismissively, 'You have no hard evidence. This is a family weekend.'

'On the contrary, we have witnesses for what has happened. The conversations as well as our video recordings from hidden cameras here in the castle.'

'That won't hold up in court.' Gunter grumbles.

'I think you'll find it will. Plus we have your brother Wilhelm who, miraculously I should say, seems to have recovered some of his memory from five years ago. He's agreed to receive further treatment for PTSD and has decided to stay in Scotland for a while to, as he says, sort himself out.'

Herr Schiltz looks defeated. 'The ring, you're here because of the ring?'

'Yes.' Inspector Joachin nods.

'So, if I hadn't bought the ring none of this would have happened?'

'The ring, as you well know, belonged to the Sultan of Dubai. It was stolen from his home by one of his staff last year and smuggled out of the country. It ended up in the hands of a Russian arms dealer, who traded it and used it for currency, for weapons, to fund the war in Syria. You, Herr Schiltz, were offered it, in return for transporting a shipment of arms.'

'That's not true.' Herr Schiltz doesn't sound convinced.

'Its value is probably over $20 million. You purchased it at a fraction of the price on the black market for $1.5million. I'm sure you must have realised the bargain you had, especially as there was no recorded documentation from the sale.'

Herr Schiltz shakes his head. 'These deals happen all the time.'

'Of course they do, but I'm a firm believer that the truth will always come out,' Inspector Joachin replies. 'That's why I do this work. I don't believe anyone is above the law, or that these beautiful...' He holds up the perfectly rare and beautiful blue diamond ring. 'Treasured artefacts should be plundered by wealthy people who have no respect for the law and believe that rules don't apply to them.'

I want to cheer and whoop. Inside my heart, I'm laughing, but I remain silent, standing at the door, speechless with a silly grin on my face. When I look at Hugo, and meet his eye, he winks at me.

* * *

After Police Scotland and the other guests have left and Mike, Gunter and Herr Schiltz are taken to the police station, Louisa, Fran and Roma leave for the airport, on the condition they return straight home to Germany.

'The German police will be waiting to take their statements,' Julie explains to me. Jim will drive them to the airport, and he'll make the journey back to London with Paula.

Before she leaves Paula hugs me, and I whisper, 'Don't be afraid.'

She looks at me strangely. 'I won't. I have nothing to fear.'

'I mean, if you're in love with Freya, don't be afraid of having a relationship.'

Her cheeks blush. 'She told you?'

I nod. 'Be happy.'

Jim looks at me over the bonnet of the car before climbing into the driver's seat. He gives me a quick salute and I'm pleased that I never had to tackle him. I'd never have won.

I watch them drive off, then I go to my room and begin to pack my overnight bag, checking to make sure I don't leave anything behind. I change out of my white tunic and bandana into cut-off jeans and a pretty blouse.

I wonder what will happen to Herr Schiltz's company, the staff and their jobs.

Who will take the helm of the business?

I guess that Paula and the lawyers will be busy, perhaps Jack will now get involved, this could even be Wilhelm's time to shine.

Perhaps he might have learned a valuable lesson, just as I have.

Before she left, Inspector Niven thanked me for my hard work. She called me a valuable asset – so now, maybe I can do anything. I'm beginning to feel more normal. As if I've regained my confidence after my disastrous relationship with James.

I'll go home, take Tina out this week to celebrate and have long runs with Molly. I'll get my business back on track. Having seen how this family turned out, I'm even brave enough to speak to James's mother. I can explain it to her. I will tell her I'm bankrupt. I will make sure James is not off the hook, and I will get my money back.

I'll get back to the top of my game.

I look around the converted stable; this poky room at Castle Calder has been my safety net.

It's not about money, as Herr Schiltz now knows. Dealing with illegal, stolen goods, whether they're imported from China or purchased on the black market, is wrong. And he'll pay the price – they all will, including Gunter and Mike, for murder.

All the family thought they were above the law and could conceal the truth; buy a stolen ring, hide a murder weapon in the bank vault, import illegal goods. But the truth comes out. You can't hide everything forever.

I add my washbag to my weekend bag and zip it shut.

I'm sure Louisa will be happy. She's still young enough to meet someone else. She wasn't aware of the value of the stolen diamond, and by all accounts, she is an innocent party, even to the murder of Herr Schiltz's first wife. They tried to conceal their affair, but everyone knew and it caused so much hypocrisy and ill will within the family.

Was it worth it?

Fran will face the German police for lying five years ago, and her husband will surely go to prison. And Roma, she will bring up the three children while Gunter is in prison. This is a prime example of how a family weekend doesn't turn out as you expect.

I take a last look around the room and check my reflection. It's the same face looking back at me, but during these few days in Scotland, I've changed.

'I'm Ronda,' I whisper. Then I smile at myself. 'And I'm back.'

I close the door of the small studio.

Julie and Mac are waiting for me outside in the evening sunlight. We hug, and I wipe away a tear.

'Why didn't you hide the gun on the table— or Hugo?' I ask.

'They may have been suspicious of Hugo or me but there's no

way anyone would ever suspect you were working for Europol – you're a *Masterchef*. Stay in touch?' she adds smiling.

'Definitely. You must come and visit me in London, with Mac, of course.' I smile at him and throw my arms around his neck too.

'Thank you both.'

'Take care, Ronda. Let us know who you're cooking for next time.' Mac grins. 'It will probably be someone very famous.'

I laugh and wave as I walk away. 'But it won't be as exciting as this weekend.'

Hugo and Inspector Joachin are waiting beside the car.

'I'm dropping Hugo at the train station for the overnight train to London. Are you sure you want to go back tonight?' Inspector Joachin asks.

'Definitely. There's been too much excitement here – enough for me to last a lifetime.'

I sling my weekend bag onto the back seat and climb into the car behind the inspector, and it allows me to study Hugo's profile.

He hasn't said much. I guess that he will be out of a job. No more sommelier work with Herr Schiltz. He may have to go back to restaurant work in France or Spain.

I realise I'm looking forward to spending eight hours on a train with him, and I hope I don't fall asleep and waste precious time.

'What will happen to Paula?' I ask.

Inspector Joachin drives the car, and he looks at me periodically in the rear-view mirror.

'She'll be out of a job now they've taken Herr Schiltz,' I add. 'If he hadn't hidden the murder weapon five years ago events might have turned out differently for all of them.'

'Paula always liked Wilhelm. He might keep her on, as it seems he's going to be the one to take over the running of the company.'

'Wilhelm?'

'He's in police custody at the moment, but he's done nothing wrong. It seems like he's the one to take the helm and lead this family forward. He's happy to work with the police and to find out the truth.'

I gaze out of the window, watching the evening lights of Aberdeen coming on and flashing by, thinking of the beating I gave him on two occasions. He doesn't seem to have made a fuss to the police about it, and for that, I feel grateful.

'What about the note?' I ask. 'The one that Iris wrote before she died, that Herr Schiltz carried in his wallet.'

Hugo replies, 'I took a photo of it.'

He takes out his phone and reads it.

'Dearest Friedrich. I know what you have done. You have betrayed me, your sons and your business. I will not rest until you pay for your crimes. I am going to the police.'

'She never got to the police, though, did she?'

'Mike arrived at the house first and he killed her. By the time Wilhelm arrived, she was dead and he was devastated. Herr Schiltz came home a few minutes later.'

'Was the note written in English?'

'Yes, Iris was American.'

'So, that's why he couldn't show the note to the police. It incriminated him.'

'Yes.' Hugo puts his phone away.

'But he didn't destroy it.'

'It must have been a constant reminder to him. He thought his son Wilhelm had killed his own mother – his wife – and he blamed himself.'

'It didn't stop him from purchasing a blue diamond illegally,' I mumble. We wait for a traffic light. 'He's a crook.'

'He's the sort of man who will never change. You know that, Ronda.' Hugo turns in his seat and regards me briefly. 'He's not a murderer but he is an awful father, as you well know.'

I'm surprised Hugo makes this reference to my father. Nothing changed him. There was no moment of regret, apology, or atonement. He simply died without paying the price for the damage he caused his wife – and me – and my younger brother. He was a bully. He never faced his day of retribution and it all seems so unfair.

I sigh.

'So, what about you, Ronda?' Inspector Joachin asks. He meets my eyes in the mirror. 'What are your plans?'

'I'm going to rebuild my business.'

He turns the car into the train station.

'We have five minutes,' Hugo says. 'Until the train leaves.'

Inspector Joachin climbs out of the car with us.

'I hope we'll see each other soon,' he says.

'Soon?' I laugh. 'Are you coming to London?'

'Perhaps. If everything works out.'

He looks at Hugo, and I give him a shy smile. Inspector Joachin must know we kissed in the garden, he knows everything else, and I'm suddenly embarrassed.

'You see, Ronda, I've been thinking. Inspector Niven was right. You're a precious asset, and you took to this work instinctively and I'm hoping that you'll give some thought to joining us.'

'Us?'

'We often work with civilians with the necessary skill sets

to help us, and you'd be a very valuable undercover, shall we say, helper?'

'I'm a chef.'

'I know. Now, go and get your train. Hugo will explain everything on your journey back to London.'

'Hugo?' I turn to look at him. 'Hugo?'

He winks at me.

'Are you a helper?'

Hugo shakes his head. 'No, I'm a police officer with Europol. That's why I had to take a back seat with the events in Castle Calder. I had to let Julie lead and make the arrest, and she did a great job.'

'You're a policeman?'

Hugo smiles. 'And a sommelier. It's just one of my undercover duties.'

I stare at him.

He had saved me that day coming out of Herr Schiltz's bedroom. He had shown me the secret passageway. He'd moved Jim's cameras and he'd kissed me in the garden. All in the name of duty?

'Right,' I say coldly, slinging my bag over my shoulder. 'Let's go. I'm not missing this train.'

Hugo and Inspector Joachin share a puzzled glance.

But I don't wait. I stride off towards the platform and to the train taking me to my newfound destiny in London.

'Duty!' I mutter, waiting on the platform. 'Duty! Sod Hugo. I never want to speak to him again. I'm going to sleep for eight hours on the train.'

The End.

Want to read more?

Read on for an extract: *The Influencers*

The Influencers
Book 2

A Ronda George Thriller
Talented kickboxer and *Masterchef* turns detective.

After a shattering discovery – will Ronda survive?

Charismatic TV personality Daniel Clarkson employs Ronda George to cater at an exclusive function in his well-known Kent country pub.

She's shocked to find her ex, James Frampton, who stole her savings, is launching a new cryptocurrency.

With the help of eight wealthy, social influencers it will take the Internet by storm.

But Ronda discovers that the business deal is a scam. James

and his business partners will stop at nothing to launch the venture - even if it means silencing her forever.

Ronda's intuition and instincts kick in and she calls on her army and martial arts skills in order to survive and get back what's rightfully hers.

The *Influencers* is the second book in the Ronda George series of thrillers which can be read and enjoyed in any order, although it's exciting to watch Ronda's personal development with each book in the series and it's preferable to read them in sequence.

Fans of female sleuths and aficionados of Lucy Foley, Catherine Cooper, Allie Reynolds, Shari Lapena, Riley Sager and Lisa Jewell.

The Influencers - Chapter 1

'One must pass through the network of influence. One is obligated to be influenced, and one accepts this influence very naturally. From the start, one doesn't realize this. The first thing to know: one doesn't realize one is influenced. One thinks he is already liberated, and one is far from it!'
Marcel Duchamp

The autumn downpour takes me by surprise, and heavy rain is trickling down my neck. I'm juggling the front door key, balancing my shopping, including tonight's dinner of lamb kebabs, and Molly's lead, when my mobile rings. I push open the door, and Molly tugs herself free. She's excited to be home, knocks against my leg and I lose my balance and my grip. My shopping drops on the floor. The fresh brown eggs smash on the concrete step.

'Hello?'

'Ronda George?' The stranger's voice is formal and shows signs of an expensive education.

'Yes.'

'Daniel Clarkson, we haven't met. I'm—'

I know precisely who Daniel Clarkson is. He's one of the most well-known celebrities you could imagine, a face for TV:

chiselled jaw, sculpted cheekbones and, even dimples. He's the nation's favourite host. He's successfully narrated a series of documentary TV programmes from rail travel across the globe to unusual gardens in Bolivia.

'I hope you don't mind me calling you, but the thing is, I own a pub in the heart of the Kent countryside ...' I hear the proud smile in his voice.

His pub, The Cockerel and the Guinea Pig is legendary. It's booked up months in advance, and it's almost impossible to get a table reservation. Tina and I have tried on many occasions since it opened three years ago, and in the end we gave up. It's often in the *Hello!* magazine with celebrity couples posing outside with their fast, flashy cars.

I'm speechless.

Daniel Clarkson is calling me.

'The thing is,' he continues in his melodic TV voice, 'my regular chef is ill, and I have a crucially important function to cater for, and I was wondering if you'd be free.'

I glance at the mess oozing out of the paper bag—the sticky eggs leaking over the doorstep. Molly stands looking hopefully at the lamb, so I nudge her away with my knee and pick it up.

I glance back into the quiet London street. It's a haven of peace in the busy metropolis, and I'm wondering if I'm on some reality show. A celebrity set-up where a reporter suddenly appears laughing saying, *'we fooled you'*, and you feel an absolute idiot while trying to smile for the cameras.

'Ronda? Are you there?'

'Yes, I am. Sorry.'

'I did see you on *Masterchef*. How many years ago was that?'

'Almost three.'

'My goodness, was it really?'

I close my eyes and rub my temple as flashing images of my life fill my head: the fame, the recognition, the media attention, the fun and laughter. Then the best part – the hard work – the challenge and the success when I was recognised for my skill and artistry in the kitchen. I was happy then, but that was before James and his betrayal—

'Have I caught you at a bad time, Ronda?'

Inside, waiting at the end of the hallway, Molly is now in her downward dog pose, tail wagging, waiting for her breakfast. She barks. It's a small yap to remind me she's had a long walk and she's hungry.

'No, it's fine.'

He hesitates, and then he gives a small embarrassed laugh.

'Um, well. Perhaps it's not something you'd like to do then?'

I'd be crazy to turn him down. It's the chance of a lifetime, to work with one of the most well-known, and revered masters of television. It's also the opportunity of a lifetime to resurrect my flailing career. Apart from catering for a wealthy German businessman a few months ago in Scotland, I can't seem to get my business kick-started again – or my confidence. This is what I need.

'I'm sorry I bothered you, Ronda. It's just that—'

'Sorry, no, no. Daniel, I'd love to. It would be a pleasure.'

Did I really call him Daniel with such familiarity?

'Great, that's fantastic.' He sounds genuinely pleased.

'Yes, I'm sorry. I know I should sound far more enthusiastic, less star-struck,' I admit with a smile that I wish he could see, and I'm rewarded with his throaty laugh. I warm to the theme and add, 'It's very kind of you to think of me. Let me check my calendar.'

I slam the front door with my foot, leaving the mess of the

uncooked scrambled eggs on the step and I lean with my back against the front door. It's beginning to dawn on me, I'm speaking to Daniel Clarkson, and he wants me to cook in his famous pub.

'When is it for?' I ask.

'Well, unfortunately, it *is* short notice. It's for this Wednesday.'

I push past Molly who can't believe I'm doing something more important than feeding her. She jumps up and puts her muddy paws on my jacket. I push her off, throw the lamb on the kitchen counter and reach for my diary. I check the date knowing my diary is empty.

'The first Wednesday in November?' I ask.

'Yes.'

'Um, I think I could juggle that around ….' I pretend. 'That would be fine, Daniel. I'll pop it in my diary.'

He breathes a solemn and dramatic sigh.

'Thank goodness for that,' he gushes. 'I thought you were going to turn me down, Ronda. You certainly know how to keep a man on his toes.'

I hear the smile in his voice, and I realise it's what makes him successful. It's what they call *charisma*, and it's what I'm lacking. After ten years in the British Army, I haven't developed these skills. Fortunately, in the kitchen, I can be monosyllabic and grumpy if I want to be, so long as I work in a team. I can lose myself in my profession as a chef. How I won *Masterchef*, or why I was so popular still remains a mystery to me.

'It's all pretty straightforward,' he explains. 'The guests are arriving at midday. They'll have coffee or aperitifs and then lunch at one-thirty.'

'That's fine.' I make a note in my diary.

'Erm, they're an international crowd. There are a few people you may recognise, you know, a few celebrities, a politician and even a prince but I'm sure you will be discreet.'

'Of course.'

I don't add that fame or the celebrity lifestyle doesn't interest me and that I'm more into good manners and kindness.

'The thing is, Ronda, no one must know about this meeting, this gathering. You will have to sign a waiver, a declaration, not to speak about it. It's standard practice in this situation. These people don't want to have their lives splashed all over the press.'

Unless it suits them and you want the Hello! *magazine all over your pub*, I want to add, but I say aloud, 'That's fine.'

'I guess you've signed something before when you've cooked for royalty?'

'Yes, something similar,' I reply.

That's why he wants me. He's heard that I've cooked for Charles and Camilla on several occasions. It's something I never speak about, but the word does get out, and I'm not complaining. After winning *Masterchef*, I'd been very successful; jetting all over the world to cook for private functions in exotic locations, for pop stars, billionaires, philanthropists, business people and even royalty. It had been thrilling, exciting and fun; however, that was over a year ago – before I lost everything – before James took everything, including my confidence.

'Good. Good. I'm delighted, Ronda. Well, I won't take up any more of your time. I'm sure you're a very busy woman. I'll send you an email confirming it all, your remuneration and, of course, the disclosure document.'

'Perfect.'

'If you have any questions just email me.'

'What about the menu?'

'It will be straightforward, very low key.'

'How many guests?'

'Eight.'

I stare at Molly, who sits watching me patiently. She's giving me her Paddington hard stare, to get me off the phone quickly.

'Eight?' I scribble down the number in my empty diary. I know that afterwards, in my excitement, I won't remember a word of what Daniel's said and I suddenly can't wait to tell Tina.

He continues, 'I'll send you the menu suggestions. I'll purchase everything fresh the day before, and I'll send you a list. If you come down early on Wednesday morning and there's anything else you need, I can always get someone to pop out and get it for you. Does that sound, alright?'

'You don't want me to suggest a menu?'

'No, not at all. The host is quite particular. I'll email you now with the details, and I'll see you on Wednesday. I'll send you directions to my place. It should only take an hour from your home.'

'You know where I live?' He doesn't answer so I say, 'Can I ask how you got my phone number and who recommended me?'

He pauses before answering.

'A very good friend, someone who thinks very highly of you.'

Tina, my best friend, is an international criminal lawyer but she would have warned me. She'd have given me the heads up that Daniel was going to phone me, besides, she's probably never even met Daniel Clarkson. So, who else could it be? I wonder if it's any of my old army companions, but I doubt it would be anyone who wouldn't forewarn me.

Molly sits at my feet, looking hopeful.

'Thinks highly of me,' I reply automatically.

'Yes, James Frampton recommended you,' Daniel says softly in my ear.

'James?' I whisper.

'Yes, he speaks very highly of you. He said that you were the one.'

My knees give way, and I slump onto the kitchen chair. My mouth is dry, and my hands are shaking. My stomach turns and lifts as if I'm on a rollercoaster and I think I may be sick.

Molly regards me warily, pads closer and then places her head on my knee, as if she's aware of my sudden distress.

'James?' I mumble.

'He'll be thrilled to know you've agreed.'

James. I feel my anger igniting. My shock has turned to fire and outrage. How dare James speak about me? I never want to see or hear from him again. I don't want anything to do with him, but I *do* want my money back. My money that he stole from me last February – almost nine months ago.

'But, he won't be as delighted as me,' Daniel purrs. 'I'm looking forward to it already.'

Janet Pywell's Books

Ronda George Thrillers:
The Concealers
The Influencers
The Manipulators
The Ronda George Thriller Boxset - books 1-3

Mikky dos Santos Thrillers:
Golden Icon – *The Prequel*
Masterpiece
Book of Hours
Stolen Script
Faking Game
Truthful Lies
Broken Windows

Boxsets
Volume 1 – Masterpiece, Book of Hours & Stolen Script
Volume 2 – Faking Game, Truthful Lies & Broken Windows

Other Books by Janet Pywell:
Red Shoes and Other Short Stories
Bedtime Reads
Ellie Bravo

For more information visit:
   website: www.janetpywell.com
   blog: janetpywellauthor.wordpress.com

All books are available online and can be ordered through major book stores.

If you enjoy my books then please do leave a review from wherever you purchased the book. Your opinion is important to me. I read them all. It also helps other readers to find my work.

Thank you.

About the Author

Author Janet Pywell's storytelling is as mesmerizing and complex as her characters.

In the Mikky dos Santos international crime thriller series - art forger, artist and photographer Mikky is a uniquely lovable female: a tough, tattooed, yet vulnerable protagonist who will steal your heart. Each book is a stand-alone exciting action-adventure novel, set in three uniquely different countries/locations.

In the first series of domestic crime thrillers, Ronda George is a kickboxing *Masterchef*. After ten years in the British Army assigned to some of the world's most dangerous places, Ronda is enlisted by Inspector Joachin García Abascal to infiltrate the murky underworld of greed, corruption and betrayal.

These books are a must-read for devotees of complex female sleuths.

Janet has a background in travel and tourism and she writes using her knowledge of foreign places gained from living abroad and travelling extensively. She currently lives on the Kent coast.

You can connect with me on:

- http://www.janetpywell.com
- https://twitter.com/JanPywellAuthor
- https://www.facebook.com/JanetPywell7227
- https://payhip.com/JanetPywell
- https://janetpywellauthor.wordpress.com

Subscribe to my newsletter:

- https://www.subscribepage.com/janetpywell

www.ingramcontent.com/pod-product-compliance
Lightning Source LLC
Chambersburg PA
CBHW061230210726
48293CB00003B/719